NEED TO KNOW

AND

OTHER STORIES

FROM

NORTH CAROLINA

by

RICHARD McLAWHORN

TRAFFORD

Publishing Inc.

Contact the author at Post Office Box 399, Grifton, NC 28530, or contact Trafford Publishing, Inc., 301 South Front Street, New Bern, NC 28560-9767.

Printed in Victoria, Canada

National Library of Canada Cataloguing in Publication

McLawhorn, Richard, 1943-
    Need to know, and other stories from North Carolina / Richard McLawhorn
ISBN 1-55395-782-2
    I. Title.
PS3613.C578N43 2003   813'.6   C2003-900743-X

TRAFFORD

This book was published *on-demand* in cooperation with Trafford Publishing. On-demand publishing is a unique process and service of making a book available for retail sale to the public taking advantage of on-demand manufacturing and Internet marketing. **On-demand publishing** includes promotions, retail sales, manufacturing, order fulfilment, accounting and collecting royalties on behalf of the author.

Suite 6E, 2333 Government St., Victoria, B.C. V8T 4P4, CANADA
Phone   250-383-6864   Toll-free   1-888-232-4444 (Canada & US)
Fax   250-383-6804   E-mail   sales@trafford.com
Web site   www.trafford.com
TRAFFORD PUBLISHING IS A DIVISION OF TRAFFORD HOLDINGS LTD.
Trafford Catalogue #03-0145   www.trafford.com/robots/03-0145.html

10   9   8

For Marian, Alex, Daphne, John, and Adam

Table of Contents

Retail managers returning from a meeting in Fayetteville, North Carolina, are detained by the police who search their car and discover drugs. The travelers claim that they were "Framed".

In "Passive Resistance", Louis Faulkner is involved with shipmate Bobby Wiesner once again, but this time the ending is different.

North Carolina State University student Graham Warf possesses an extraordinary gift that has caught the attention of the United States security establishment. The gift is a powerful one, but in many ways it is a burden. "Need to Know" is the story of how Graham and his two best friends deal with the secret.

THE VISITOR

Wallace liked to make up stories. Funny, weird, and unusual stories. Wallace had entertained family, teachers, and friends for years, and now he had begun to write his stories down. He wrote about ordinary people who were visited by aliens or who searched for friends who disappeared without a trace. He wrote about people with the power to read the minds of others. His parents' co-workers sent home names of magazines and publishers' addresses for Wallace to contact. He could be the next Stephen King, they said. That's why it just wasn't fair for him to be all alone when it happened.

The date was April second. That was easy to remember because the day before had been one of Wallace's favorite days of the year. He always played some very original tricks on April Fools Day, and this year had been one of his best efforts. He had run a help-wanted newspaper advertisement offering a position as school janitor. The pay was twenty dollars an hour. The phone in the office at the high school had rung every thirty seconds. No one knew who was responsible. No one except several hundred of Wallace's friends.

Otherwise, it had been an unremarkable day, a cloudy, blustery spring day. Home from school, Wallace sucked on a chocolate-covered popsicle as he sat before his computer and prepared to check his e-mail. From his window on the second floor he watched the live oaks that lined the street sway and dance as they anticipated the rain which now began to tap softly on the ancient tin roof of the Patterson home. Wallace had the big house to himself today. Kristen, his twin sister, had walked home with her friend Patty, and Victor, the twelve-year-old, had baseball practice.

Wallace was typing his password when an explosion shook the floor of his house and rattled the window next to his desk. Wallace hesitated, then sprang to his feet, his thoughts racing ahead so that his physical movement toward the window seemed to be in slow motion, dream-like. This can not be happening, he thought. A bomb, he thought, it's the Michigan Militia or the Iranians. Maybe the Air Force dropped one by mistake. Nothing out back. Check the side yard. Nothing. He bounded down the stairs, his heart pounding in his ears. What if there were more bombs? Out the door, across the yard, still no fire or damage in sight. Wait. There it was. A hint of smoke drifting over from the Rasberrys' house next door. No one would be at home; both Phil and Marcy Rasberry were at work, David had joined the navy, and Kevin was away at UNC.

Around back, he found what he had been looking for. Above his head in the wall of his neighbors' house loomed a large hole framed by dangling strands of plaster, pink insulation, and vinyl siding. What was that strange object protruding from the opening? He tried the back door. Locked, of course. Should he break the glass? Glancing around, he spotted the aluminum extension ladder suspended from two hooks on the wall of the shed. A few moments later the ladder was in place against the house, and he scrambled up to have a look. The smoke parted to reveal what appeared to be a space capsule. Wallace froze.

A crack appeared in the hull of the spacecraft. A

small door swung open and a human face appeared at the opening.

"Har gaidy biet lod?" the man asked.

Wallace's head reeled.

"Wroom hoor thret? Harret airy esty et?" the astronaut tried again.

The dark face of the lively stranger wore a broad smile and his wide-eyed stare shifted from Wallace to the contents of the room, back to Wallace, to the a view of the outside though the window beyond the bed. It was obvious that the newcomer and the dark-haired young man on the ladder were equally excited.

"Wait," Wallace finally answered, "I can't understand you. Do you speak English?"

The creature held up one finger and ducked back into the capsule. When he emerged a few moments later, he wore a bright red helmet that resembled the hard hats worn by construction workers.

"What year is it?" the man asked.

"1998. Where did you come from? How did you get here?"

"Jiminy! It happened! Success at last! Would you please assist me, my young friend? I can't seem to get the door open any wider."

"You're wedged up against the dresser."

"Dresser, eh? What is a dresser?"

"This is Mr. and Mrs. Rasberry's bedroom. The dresser is where they keep their underwear and socks. Where are you from?"

"All in good time, my friend," answered the man in the helmet. "Climb up here and slide my ship away from the dresser, if you please."

Wallace did as he was asked, and he found the capsule to be much lighter than it looked. The stranger climbed out and stretched. He was wearing a bright red space suit. Smiling, he held out a gloved hand. He seemed pleased with himself that he knew how to shake hands. The boy, well over six feet tall, reached down and squeezed the small hand with his long, bony fingers.

Wallace was thinking that if he had made up this story, he would certainly not have had the visitor wear that hideous red suit. The outfit somehow made the visitor look less credible, almost comical. And his small stature didn't help any.

"What is that intimidating sound? We are not in danger, are we?"

"Sound?...Oh, the dog!" Wallace suddenly became aware of the frantic barking of Brandy, the cocker spaniel confined in the kitchen downstairs.

"Dog?"

"A pet. Downstairs. She can't get up here. She's locked in the kitchen."

"Pardon me, but what is a pet?"

"An animal that we keep and feed and care for. Sometimes they're like members of the family."

"Very strange. Ah, please allow me to introduce myself. My name is Hoonzig," he said.

"Mine's Wallace. Wallace Patterson. Where did you come from?"

"I'll answer all your questions, young man, but I'm afraid you will not believe me, and neither will your parents nor the authorities that they are sure to summon. Please help me to remove my ship from this dwelling and to conceal it temporarily in a secure location."

Wallace did not know exactly why he was helping the man, but he ran over to his house, removed the truck key from the hook, and backed his dad's pickup into the Rasberrys' yard. The capsule was too large to fit through the bedroom door, so Hoonzig began to disassemble the strange vehicle. Wallace had enticed the dog to the den with a bowl filled with Alpo. She had finally stopped barking. The pair carried the pieces of the spacecraft down the stairs and out the back door to place them in the bed of the pickup. As they left the bedroom, Hoonzig inquired about the material from which the dresser was made.

"Wood," Wallace told him.

4

"I was hoping that was the case," he said. He removed a glove and fondly stroked the edge of the dresser.

Wallace drove through the back streets and down a dirt road to his grandfather's farm.

"Is everyone on your planet short?"

"Yes, we plan it that way. We eat less and we save on building costs because our ceilings can be lower."

"Are people with dark skin treated okay there?"

"I'm sorry, I don't understand the question." He paused, his hand on the side of his helmet.

"Oh, yes, very interesting question. Yes, all people are treated the same, without regard to their genetic makeup. As a matter of fact, racial differences is no longer a topic of conversation. I'm not sure that my contemporaries are conscious of the differences. People are just people, all short."

"How long have you been traveling?"

"For centuries."

Wallace glanced at him, puzzled. He slowed the truck and turned at an abandoned farm house, and they bounced along a narrow farm path that led them to a wooded area in the distance. The land on either side, freshly cultivated and ready for planting, stretched to the trees that lined the banks of the drainage canals in the distance. The threat of rain had passed, and the late afternoon sun was making an appearance.

They spotted Carl Hodges with two other men, in the distance, working on the tobacco beds. If weather conditions were favorable, they would be pulling the plants the following week and transplanting them. Carl had been renting the Patterson land since Wallace was a small boy. Unlike many of the local farmers who raised their tobacco plants in greenhouses, Carl still produced his in the long, plastic-covered plant beds located adjacent to the woods for protection from the wind. When he looked up and recognized the pickup, the farmer grinned and waved to his young friend before returning to his work.

5

Wallace and Hoonzig hid the ship in an abandoned tobacco barn, nestled with four others, leaning and sagging with age, in a cluster of tall pine trees. They rode back down the path in silence. They were back on the main highway when Wallace's small companion began his story.

"Wallace, my new friend, I must explain who I am. I know that you will find this difficult to comprehend, but I am human, an earthling. I come from the future."

"You are kidding!" Wallace ran off the road and almost lost control. He drove into the Trade Mart parking lot and applied the brakes, almost throwing his passenger into the dashboard.

"Come on, Mister, please don't kid around like that! It's like one of my stories!"

"I assure you, young Wallace, I am indeed what I claim to be. And thank you for your enthusiasm. I can hardly contain my excitement. You see, I am the world's first time traveler!"

"Holy moley! What century do you come from?"

"Time is measured differently in my time than in yours. However, if my calculations are correct, I have traveled back three thousand four hundred and thirty-one years."

Wallace decided that someone was playing an elaborate trick on him. Who was in on it? Mom and Dad? The Rasberrys? Surely his cousin Tom had planned it. Tom was fourteen months older than Wallace was, and the two had been best friends since birth. Wallace had to admit, Mr. Wise Guy had really gotten his goat this time. Payback would have to be something outrageous.

"How much did they pay you to do this? Are you a professional actor?"

Puzzled, Hoonzig pulled on his helmet and listened intently for a few seconds, then he responded with a hearty laugh.

"Wallace, I am not surprised that you don't believe me. I would react the same way were I in your place. Let me think. You haven't explored or even visited Mars or

6

Venus yet, is that correct? I wish I had taken the time to read more history of the 1990's. I did not do so because I had not intended to stop here."

"Do you still have drugs and crime and poverty in the future? How about cancer and AIDS?" asked Wallace.

"Oh, no, my young friend. I am a scholar and ancient history is among my many interests. I understand these problems that you have mentioned. You see, you are living in what will be known as the Age of Scarcity. In our century, we have no scarcity, no diseases, and very little crime. You are very gracious to help me here, in your time, but in my world, I would expect it. And you would assist me without hesitation. You see, in the future, everyone has everything he or she needs. If we find someone who needs something, we are eager to help them fill that need."

"Amazing, how did you ... will you do it? What happened to the Age of Scarcity?"

"Technology, my friend. Technology has solved all our problems. To be more precise, we have none of those problems on earth. They re-emerge occasionally on some of our colonies. In my time, we have colonies on all the planets except Mercury, Neptune, and Pluto. And on many of the moons."

"Do we have people on planets outside the solar system?"

"No. Well, maybe. Several groups have departed, but we have not heard from any of them. We have not learned to travel faster than the speed of light."

"Where have you been? What years?"

"Wallace, that will take a considerable amount of time to explain. Can we get some nourishment? We have not changed so much in all this time. We still get hungry five times each day. And I haven't eaten in centuries."

Wallace started the engine and eased the pickup out to the street.

"How about Burger King?"

"Whatever that is, it sounds delicious."

Could this guy be real? His emotions, his mannerisms, his humanness, even his corny sense of humor were so contemporary. Could it be that people had changed so little in all those thousands of years? Wallace was having a hard time swallowing this guy's story.

Hoonzig hated Burger King. He didn't say so, but he didn't eat more than a few bites of anything Wallace brought him. He didn't even like the water.

"By the way, do you have more than one name? Mine is Wallace Patterson. Wallace Edward Patterson."

"My name is Hoonzig Rinny-Frun," answered the dark little man, smiling.

If he was for real, his presence needed to be concealed, for the time being, anyway.

"We need to find somewhere for you to stay," Wallace said. "It's getting late. When my parents get home they'll wonder where I am. A hotel. We'll go to Masonboro and find you a hotel room."

"Hotel?"

"We'll need money for that."

"Money?"

"Or a credit card. Don't ask. I'll explain later."

There were a couple of credit cards at home in the cabinet above the telephone, some that his mother kept to use while they were on vacation. He glanced at his watch. Fifteen minutes before his mother would be home. He turned the corner and accelerated. Kristen or Victor might be there. He'd have to make it quick.

He swung into his driveway and leaped out of the truck.

"Wait here. I'll be right back."

He got lucky. He was in and out of the house in a flash. No one was around. He had the card in his pocket. Thirty minutes later they were in a room at the Ramada Inn. Wallace called home to tell them that he was in Masonboro and would be home soon. Kristen had answered the phone, and she didn't ask any questions. Wallace then walked across the street to the Food Lion and bought Hoonzig two bagels, a can of peanuts, some apples, and a

8

quart of orange juice. The little visitor, after cautiously sampling each item, grinned and nodded his approval. He consumed generous amounts of the food as he sat on the bed and watched television, spellbound.

After his snack, Hoonzig looked tired, but he insisted on telling his story.

"For more than a century we have had the capability to travel in time, but we traveled only as observers. It is strange and hard to explain. One can guide his ship to any location at any moment in the past or future, but he can not communicate with the people at these locations. The time traveler is in a different dimensional plane from that of the environment being visited."

"You mean you are like a ghost or something?"

"Exactly. Very good."

"Then how did you arrive here, in the flesh?"

"All in good time, my friend. First, I retired three years ago. I was a scientist, a chemist. I had traveled through time before, but, as a retired senior citizen, time travel has become an obsession. Oh, I have visited so many magic moments in history. I have witnessed our destiny, so many millennia in the distant future. It was natural, I suppose, that I soon found myself experimenting with the possibility of entering the plane of the visited sites. Well, in a nutshell, I apparently succeeded, and here I am. I must admit I'm almost as shocked as you are. I'd like to spend a few days here, if possible, and then I'll relieve you of the burden of my presence. Provided, of course, that I can duplicate my settings, in reverse."

"You are serious, aren't you? How old are you?"

"Two hundred and seventy-seven years of age. Our average life span is now about three hundred to three twenty."

"Amazing."

Suddenly Hoonzig's expression changed from one of good cheer to one of serious concentration. He was silent for a few moments, then he sprang to his feet in obvious alarm.

"Oh, my Diety! We must return to the ship immediately! Please!"

Hoonzig's sudden movement and the frantic expression on his face unnerved his young companion.

"Sure! What is it? What did you forget?"

"How could I be so stupid? In all the excitement, I just wasn't thinking. Of all the chances I took and dangers I faced in coming here, one of the worst and most obvious are the microorganisms. I have no immunity! We have no disease in my century. I have never even seen a sick person. I feel like such an old fool."

"Well, let's go, sir." They were in the truck by now. Wallace drove as quickly as he could, but he didn't want to speed and draw attention.

"Do you have medication on your ship?" he asked.

"Yes. I have a complete medical kit and a space suit on board. How could I forget the need for them?"

"Don't be so hard on yourself. You had a right to be excited. You've done something no human has done before."

Hoonzig looked at his young friend and smiled. A weak smile. He doesn't look too good, Wallace thought to himself.

The sun had set, and a pink sky loomed ahead as they drove westward. Wallace switched on the headlights, but he turned them off when he turned into the farm path that led to the old barns in the grove of pines. When the truck skidded to a stop, Wallace hopped out and hurried around to assist Hoonzig who was now too weak to move on his own. Wallace found a flashlight in the glove compartment of the truck, and the two, after reaching the interior of the old barn, picked through the components of the time capsule until they found the compartment where the medical supplies were stored. The little man removed a small pistol-like device and shot himself three times in his leg. He looked up at Wallace and smiled.

"I'll be as good as new in a Mercury minute," he said.

Wallace laughed.

Fifteen minutes later they had reassembled the ship and it stood, poised for action, a ghostly shape in the pale moonlight. Hoonzig seemed his former self, as he had promised.

"Goodbye, young Wallace. I regret that we don't have more time. There was so much I wanted to share with you."

Wallace took a deep breath, then exhaled and spoke.

"Hoonzig, I want to come with you. Please. You have no idea how much I have dreamed and longed for an experience like this."

"Wallace, I am an old man, an amateur. It's not safe. It's just an experiment. It is possible, even likely, that I could not find my way back here."

"I don't care. If I knew for sure that I would die, I would still want to go."

Hoonzig studied his young friend. He seemed a little surprised and somewhat pleased at Wallace's words.

Finally, the old man said, "I understand. There have always been people like us. I know how you feel. Come, my young pioneer. Climb in. Let us go for a ride."

It was a little cramped. Wallace had to sit on the storage compartment behind the driver's seat. The inside of the ship lit up as the man from the future began to push levers and press buttons. A low roaring sound grew to a high-pitched whine as the lights on the control panel turned green and blue. Soon the truck began to move past them. Then other objects moved past them. There were houses, automobiles, people, trees, tall buildings, all moving faster and faster. It all became a blur, and then a white light.

Then they were moving through space, moving toward the moon. They slowed as they neared the moon's surface. Down below at the center of a large crater was a spaceship, stark white, resting on the surface. A man crawled, snail-like, through the opening that had just appeared and down the ladder to the dusty crater floor. A tentative walk soon became a leaping motion, and then the astronaut was bounding along, growing more bold with each giant step.

"1969," said Wallace.

"Very good."

Wallace studied his fellow traveler. Wearing an expression of sheer joy, the diminutive pilot pressed buttons and glanced at the gauges, adjusting the settings, his tiny fingers flying about like those of a pianist. There were no apparent ill effects from the attack of the microbes.

They were on the move once more. As the vehicle began to spin, the white light returned, but the ship made no sound. The ship slowed and hovered above a city, part of which, Wallace noted, was in ruins. Blackened chimneys and crumbled brick walls, smoldering, lined the sides of some streets like crumbled tombstones waiting to tell of death and destruction. The acrid smoke that hovered above the piles of rubble repulsed young Wallace. He told himself that this must be the smell of death.

We must be in Europe, during World War II, he thought. But the object of the gathering crowd's attention, the horses and their riders that painstakingly made their way up the main thoroughfare, belonged to a different era. As the riders approached, Wallace could see that they were black soldiers in bright blue uniforms proceeding up the street in close formation. In the lead was the proud bearer of the flag of the United States. He drew impassioned applause from the growing multitude of bystanders. A large company of shoddily dressed black men, women, and children, apparently ex-slaves, marched abreast of the mounted soldiers. Next came an open carriage pulled by two pairs of beautiful white horses. Standing in the rear of the carriage was a tall, thin figure dressed in black. The hand he waved held a tall stovepipe hat. The roar from the crowd drowned out all other sounds.

"Lincoln. Richmond, April, 1865. He will be dead within a week," declared Wallace.

"Very impressive, my young scholar."

"Too bad we can't pick up John Wilkes Booth and drop him off on the moon."

Hoonzig made no reply.

They moved on. They saw Napoleon, a magnificent figure at the head of his proud army, on the march to new conquests. They witnessed Julius Caesar's invasion of Britain. Next came the fascinating operation of thousands of workers engaged in the construction of one of the great pyramids of ancient Egypt. Then the two travelers visited the extraordinary world ruled by giant dinosaurs. Wallace's head spun.

They studied the dinosaurs, fascinated by the sights and sounds and smells of this alien world. Wallace glanced at his watch, then laughed at himself. He had no idea how long they had been sightseeing. What does it really matter, he thought. We can return to the instant we departed and no time at all will have elapsed. Wallace had not felt hungry or thirsty since their departure. And fortunately he had not needed to use the bathroom. There was no facility aboard the tiny craft. It was a spooky feeling, as if he had brought along his consciousness but left his body behind.

Hoonzig reversed the direction of their journey and moved the ship into the future. Wallace witnessed the rapid expansion of urbanization on the surface of the earth. They visited a large colony, one of many, on the surface of Venus. Back on earth, there were colonies on the continent of Antarctica. There were colonies in all the oceans, some on the ocean floor and some afloat. There were people everywhere. Poverty and disease had been eliminated, and everyone lived a long and happy life. No one needed to work for a living anymore, but everyone did because they wanted to contribute, to satisfy a need.

Some things had not changed. People still played cards, watched television, went bowling, and drank wine. They also played several games that resembled tennis, handball, soccer, and baseball. Some people still lived in families. Big brothers still teased younger sisters, and

13

wives and husbands still had marital disagreements. And, as Hoonzig had explained earlier, everyone was short.

Wallace was disappointed when Hoonzig signaled that he was ready to return. The young man was aware that he had witnessed sights never seen by any other human of his time, yet there were so much more he wanted to see. He felt that he could spend the rest of his life on this journey.

Wallace had a few last requests, which Hoonzig gladly granted. The young adventurer had some ideas, ideas that, if they worked, could add spice to his life and to the lives of his family in the future. The old man was greatly amused at the audacity of his young companion.

The final stop was at the home of Wallace's grandparents. His father's mother, a favorite among all his siblings and cousins, died suddenly when Wallace was eleven. He wanted to see her again. And suddenly there she was, scolding Wallace's father, a pint-size ruffian of ten, for making Aunt Helen cry. Helen's tormentor was pretending to drop several week-old puppies into the water trough. Wallace's grandmother was pregnant. She was on her way out to the clothes line with a large basket of wet clothes. The wind danced in her auburn hair. She was tall and slightly stooped. She looked tired. He wanted to give her a big hug. What a wonderful woman. How strange. He knew the exact year she would be diagnosed with breast cancer. She would be gone just seven months after it was discovered. What an undignified way to go, at the young age of sixty-three. Wallace knew what her future held, but he was powerless to do anything about it. What a helpless feeling.

Hoonzig was ready to attempt re-entry into the "world of life", as he called it. Another session of the whirling and the bright white light, and they were in the coastal plains of North Carolina once more.

"This should be it."

The tiny ship was directed to the Patterson farm and the grove of pine trees that hid the abandoned barns.

They passed the Food Lion and Hardee's at the shopping center. Out on the four-lane, a hand full of Japanese automobiles and pickup trucks waited for the light to change. Wallace seemed to be back home.

"Why did you pick the Rasberrys' house the first time?"

"I intended to be there only a short period of time. Honestly, I did not truly believe that I would enter your world. On the chance that I did, however, I reasoned that I would not be detected inside a dwelling. I knew that the owners were not at home and that they had a large variety of foodstuffs in their refrigerator. The force of entry must have shifted me onto the wall.

"It is time to try once again, young Wallace. Please allow me to say that I have become very fond of you during our short time together. Please secure yourself as much as possible."

"I'm ready when you are."

"Hold tightly."

There was a violent tremble followed by a lurch that threw Wallace against the side of the ship. Then it was over. He had expected an explosion, but there had been none. Hoonzig swung the hatch open. Silence. No birds, no insects. The noise caused by their re-entry must have preceded them. There was a faint smell in the air, as before. Like the way your brakes smelled when you drove an automobile down a mountain. Hoon-zig reached in to assist Wallace in transferring his gangly frame through the small opening in the capsule.

"You are bleeding. Allow me to administer medication," said the old man.

"It's just a small scratch. I'll take care of it when I get home...but, what about the bacteria? You may need to medicate yourself, or whatever you do, and make a quick exit."

"Yes, you are absolutely right, young friend. Allow me to shake your hand one more time and bid farewell." His voice sounded sad.

15

Wallace embraced the little man instead.

"You can come back and visit any time, no pun intended."

"I'm afraid not. These microbes could mean disaster for my world. I fear I must make a visit to a point near the sun in order to destroy them. I would not tell you of this decision, but I don't want you to spend the rest of your life waiting for my return. Goodbye, young Wallace. It is indeed a comfort to know that my people are descended from delightful individuals such as you."

"No, you can't do that! ... All your technology! Surely there is another solution! You did it! You are the first! A pioneer!"

He clutched the little man's sleeves. Hoonzig made no reply. They embraced once more. Wallace could not speak. Hoonzig crawled inside, bolted the hatch, and was gone in a flash that pushed Wallace back with such force that he tumbled into the pine straw. Rising, he brushed the seat of his pants and looked at his watch. He was right on time.

He tried not to cry as he drove the pickup truck home, but his eyes kept watering. He should have been the most excited sixteen-year-old on the planet, but he thought he must be the most miserable. He had the big house to himself when he arrived there. In his room, he tried unsuccessfully to concentrate on his e-mail. Finally, he gave up and went down to the kitchen for a Pepsi and whatever he could find to eat. He ran his hand over his neck. The scratch was still there.

Wallace tried to tell about his experience, but, of course, no one believed him. He told Kristen, his twin sister, and he told Tom, his cousin and best friend. Both laughed and refused to listen. So Wallace didn't tell anyone else. He might have started to doubt it himself but for two factors. One was the small scar on his neck that he looked for almost every morning with the help of a hand-held mirror. The other was the mysterious hole in the side of the Rasberrys' home. The insurance company was reluctant to pay the repair bill, but they did, finally. The Rasberrys and their house and their dog made the front page of the local newspaper. There were dozens of solutions offered, from burglars with sledge hammers to a blast from a bazooka. The mystery was never solved.

***

When the VTP buzzed at seven o'clock on the morning of the tenth of July, 2016, Wallace had already showered and shaved and finished his orange juice. He was expecting the call.

Halley, Wallace's wife answered.

"It's Kristen and Greg! They're in their hotel room in Las Vegas!"

Wallace, Halley, and the two little ones gathered around the screen to hear Kristen's news. This should have been the week of the annual week-long family get together at the home of Wallace and Halley in Southport. It was necessary to postpone the occasion, however, because of the actions of Wallace's twin sister, Kristen. She had risen from her bed early one morning the week before and booked Greg and herself on a package flight to Las Vegas. The package included three days at Hotel Bellagio on the strip. She could not explain her actions.

Today was the third day of their trip. When the picture appeared on the screen, Kristen and Greg were beaming.

"We won over three hundred thousand dollars!" Kristen blurted, when she saw Wallace and his family on the screen.

"It was incredible!" Greg was equally excited. "She knew what the cards would be before they came up!"

"We were asked to leave three casinos!" Kristen exclaimed. "I knew what the dice would be before they were rolled! When we started losing, we quit. We're flying home tomorrow as planned."

"Is this a joke?" Halley wanted to know.

17

"Where are the boys?" asked Wallace and Halley's oldest daughter.

"Are you going to come to visit us this year?" asked the youngest, a pint-size imp named Grace.

"What will you do with it?" asked Halley.

Greg laughed. Kristen joined in. Soon all the Pattersons were laughing, also. They couldn't seem to stop.

"The kids are in Asheville with the neighbors, honey. Yes, Gracie, we are coming, week after next. How is mom?"

"She's fine. I talked to her last night." Wallace replied. "Listen, thank you for calling and sharing your good news. We are real happy for you. Have a good flight back, and we'll see you week after next."

On his way to work that morning, and, throughout the day, it was hard for Wallace to think about anything except his sister's joy and the happiness that her windfall would bring to her and her family. They were good people, but like most public school teachers, they were certainly not wealthy.

Wallace smiled to himself. He had known exactly when they would call. He knew how much they had won because he had been there to help them win it so many years ago.

Twins, he thought. What was it about that relationship? Why had she gotten his messages from that shadowy world where he and Hoonzig had hovered when neither Tom nor young Victor had received it? Four years ago, Kristen had bet five hundred dollars on the World Series. She could not explain her uncharacteristic action. She placed the bet when the playoffs started, when there were still twelve teams in the running. It paid her thirty-two thousand dollars. And now the trip to Las Vegas. Wallace wished Hoonzig were here to share the fun. He would have gotten a big kick out of it.

Wallace couldn't wait until the 2022 Kentucky Derby. The winner would pay thirty to one.

18

THE HESSIANS

Daniel

My name is Daniel Metzinger. I want to tell you about what happened at our home in the backcountry of North Carolina in 1781. It was a day in February that started out cold in the early morning but warmed up as the sun rose in the sky. I was ten years old at the time. I was out hunting, as usual. There is not much else to do out here in the winter. I had loaded the musket with bird shot and was out looking for quail.

I was inching through the edge of the woods when I heard my dog, Tiger, bark several times, and then I heard a rifle shot. I started to run in that direction, but I tripped and fell, hard. I landed in a thick layer of leaves in a grove of big hardwood trees up on the ridge. I reached for my musket, but I couldn't find it. When I turned over, I couldn't get up because there was the sharp point of a wicked-looking bayonet about one inch from my neck. The bayonet was attached to a long musket that was in the grasp of two giant hands way up at the other end. The cold blue eyes that peered down the barrel were set in a grim

19

face that belonged to a huge man dressed in bright red. The tall, gold helmet on his head sparkled in the sun. He shouted something that I couldn't understand. I don't mind telling you that I was scared stiff.

Before long four or five more giants came running, the tails of their red coats flapping and their helmets bobbing on their heads. They gathered around and peered down at me and chattered and laughed and discussed my predicament in a language that I soon realized was German. Some words sounded familiar, such as *der Junge*, which I knew meant "the boy." These words were used occasionally by my grandmother who grew up in Germany.

My grandmother is my mother's mother. She lives with us. My father's family was also from Germany, but I never heard him speak much German.

As my pounding heart slowed down a little and my mind started working, I realized that these men were British soldiers. We had heard that the British were on the way up from South Carolina in pursuit of General Greene and his North Carolina militia, but I never expected to actually see one. And why were these soldiers from England speaking German instead of English? One of the soldiers grabbed my arm and pulled me to my feet. Tiger, who had sneaked up to about thirty feet away, growled and barked. One of the soldiers raised his rifle, but I shouted and ran toward the dog.

"Hush, Tiger! Good dog. Don't make 'em shoot you."

"*Kamerads, komme! aussehe!*" Another soldier was calling from the top of the hill. When we reached the place where he stood, he pointed to a column of smoke just over the next hill. My heart leaped and began to pound once again, for I knew the smoke was coming from our cabin. Today was washday and the smoke was coming from the fire that heated the big black wash pot where Mama and Grandmama were scrubbing the family's clothes in our yard. I was filled with dread as we marched down the hill in that direction. Tiger followed us in the distance.

Helga

My name is Helga Metzinger. I want to tell you about what happened to my family one day when I was eight years old. My daddy was gone off to war. He was with General Washington fighting the British up in New York. That morning I was helping Grandmama feed the chickens while Mama was building the fire out in the yard for doing the wash. Daniel had gone hunting, and Aunt Ursula had gone out to check the cows to see if we had any new baby calves and to look for some early wild flowers.

Suddenly, we heard Mama call out, almost a shriek, "Daniel!"

Grandmama jumped and was off like a shot. She dashed around the smoke-house, and I caught her only when she had stopped at my mother's side. When we looked up the hill where she was pointing, we saw six giant soldiers in red-and-white uniforms and tall, gold colored helmets coming toward us with a small boy that we knew had to be Daniel. We stood and stared for a few moments, stunned. Then Mama charged out to meet them. She lost her scarf on the way out there, and, with her curly blond hair bouncing around in every direction, she appeared to be some type of wild creature, on the attack. Mama is a tall woman, kind of slender, and she can run pretty fast when she wants to. So it didn't take her long to get to Daniel. When she did, she fell to her knees and hugged him, then she sprang to her feet, grasped his arm, and towed him back in our direction. Tiger circled the soldiers, barking, to catch up with Mama and Daniel. When they reached the spot where we stood, Daniel, out of breath, managed to call out, "Grandma, they speak German!"

The soldiers paused out by the sycamore tree. Grandmama studied them briefly and then made a beeline out there to talk to them. She is a lively old woman, but she is short and stooped from all those years of hard work. The soldiers waited to see what she wanted. I stayed where I was, but I could see that they were excited when they heard Grandmama's German. They had removed their helmets and were bowing to her as they introduced themselves. They stood out there and talked for a long time. Grandmama was laughing, something she did a lot, anyway.

Finally they all came strolling up to the barn near where I was standing. She was arm-in-arm with one of the soldiers. She only came up to a little above his waist. Later we discovered that all the young men were poor Germans who had joined the British army to see the world and to make some money. All of them were from a part of Germany called Hesse, except the one Grandmama had by the arm. He was from Saxony, just like Grandmama and her family.

Mama was calling, "Joshua! Helga! Helga, you and Joshua come in this house this minute!"

Joshua, my little brother, was around by the back steps with one of the new kittens in each hand. I took his arm and we went in. I didn't want Mama to come out for us in the mood she was in. She and Daniel were inside watching the soldiers through the window. She did not like them being in her yard. They were the enemies of her husband, my daddy. Mama hadn't heard from Daddy in almost a year, and she was worried about him. We all were. Grandmama had served them a drink of water from the buckets that had been carried up from the stream earlier that morning. A few minutes later she hurried into the house to cook them some breakfast.

"Daniel," she called, "Run out to the smoke house and bring a ham. And bring a few pieces of wood for the stove. I'm going to cook some eggs."

"Mama, how can you? They're British soldiers! They're the enemy!"

Grandma seemed surprised at her daughter's outburst.

"Gretchen, my angel," she replied, "They're just young boys a long way from home. They're our country-men. They help the British only for the money."

"Mama, one of them may shoot the ball that kills Will!"

"Angel, your brave husband is five hundred miles away."

Grandmama pushed her way through the door with a pot of coffee and some cups. She was serving the soldiers who were seated around our big outdoor table under the oak tree. Suddenly, they were all on their feet, looking out past the barn. They stood, motionless, all six with their mouths open. They looked like they saw a ghost!

I peered out to see what they were gawking at, but all I saw was Aunt Ursula, walking in from the woods with a basket full of yellow daffodils. She wore a pair of tight-fitting buckskins and her short cloak with the hood, which was pushed back off her head. She is tall, like Mama, and blond, but she is not quite as slender. Her golden hair was parted in the middle and her two long pigtails hung from either side of her head. When she turned her head, I could see that she was wearing a smile, probably the broadest that I ever saw on her face.

After introductions all around and a lot of bowing and hand-kissing, Ursula sat in the yard with the young soldiers and shared the eggs, ham, and hot biscuits that Grandmama had served along with butter, fig jam, and cold milk. They laughed and had such a good time that Daniel and Joshua and I felt comfortable enough to venture outside and join in the activities there. Soon one of the soldiers reached down and sat me on his knee. Mama stayed in the house the whole time.

I didn't know Aunt Ursula knew so much German. She talked almost as much as Grandmama did. I had never seen her so excited. Her face was flushed and she still wore that big smile. The soldiers couldn't take their eyes off her. Especially the tall slim one with black hair called Klaus.

23

Hans

My name is Hans Muller. I want to tell you about what happened to my friend Klaus Braun while we were down in North Carolina. It was the winter of 1781. We had been marching with General Cornwallis' army all the way from South Carolina in hot pursuit of the rebel army, led by General Nathanael Greene. Greene was a wily old fox. He would not turn and fight because he knew that he was outnumbered and that his inexperienced troops would be no match for the British army. We were, after all, the most powerful fighting force on earth.

Twice we had all but caught the rebels, but they narrowly escaped each time, crossing the river as we stood and watched. They had burned all boats they didn't use, and we were forced to march in search of some place shallow enough for us to cross.

When we finally halted to camp for a few days and forage for food, Klaus, Kurt, Albert, Heiner, Karl, and I set out in search for a deer or some farmer's pig. It was a glorious morning, somewhat cool. We had walked a good distance when we were set upon by a barking dog. Soon Kurt discovered the dog's master, a young boy of ten.

We took the boy to his family's home, a little cabin on the bank of a bubbling stream that meandered through a small brown meadow. And would you believe it? We were pleased to discover that the boy's grandmother was born and grew up in Saxony. She actually knew some of Heiner's relatives. Her name was Frau Becker, and my God, could she cook! We stayed all day and ate like we had not eaten in weeks. She gave us a ham, sausage, and bread to take with us when we departed. The old lady was a delight. We laughed all day as she told one story after another of her experiences in the old country and on the American frontier. But the best part was that she had two beautiful daughters. One was the boy's mother. She was the wife of a rebel, a soldier in George Washington's army in New York. She remained inside their cabin all day. It

24

was the younger daughter, Ursula, that became a problem. She was sixteen at the time, three years younger than Klaus and me. She was tall, with honey-colored hair that she wore in two long pigtails. Her smile lit up her face and lifted our spirits. Her German was not good, but she spoke it with a charming accent that amused us all.

I don't know exactly when we began to notice the strange behavior of our friend Klaus, but it soon became very clear that Klaus was struck by Ursula as if she had cast a spell on him. He was at her side all afternoon, watching her every move and laughing whenever she spoke.

As we ate Frau Becker's cooking, we listened to her stories from the old country and told tall tales of our own. We sang German folk songs, which we call *Volks-lieds*. The two grandchildren soon came out and joined in the merrymaking.

"Well, lads, the sun tells me its time to head back to camp," Albert said in German. "We don't want to get caught in the forest in the dark."

"You are so right, Albert, my good friend," said Heiner. "*dang-ke ee-nen*, Frau Becker. Thank you for a lovely day. How can we repay your kindness to us?"

The old lady smiled and said in German, "The pleasure was all mine. Having you young gentlemen around me brings back many old memories of our homeland. If you can stay, you are welcome to sleep in our barn tonight."

"Your kindness is greatly appreciated, but we must return. We may be moving out in the morning."

Then Klaus cleared his throat and spoke quietly, "I'm staying."

Everyone stopped talking. We looked at Klaus, who could only stare into the eyes of Ursula. Her eyes were locked on his, her demeanor more serious now.

"I'll stay with Klaus," I offered. "We'll catch up in the morning."

Our friends tried to persuade Klaus to return to camp with us, but it was no use. We had never seen Klaus like this. When the others departed, they promised to come for us if the regiment moved out.

After the others had disappeared in the mist, Klaus and Ursula went for a walk. The temperature began to drop, and Frau Becker and her grandchildren gathered up the remains of our feast and prepared to move to the warmth of their cabin. I did not want to face the mother, Frau Metzinger. I knew that she hated us because we were British soldiers. I went into the barn to wait for Klaus. Frau Becker brought me more delicious food, a lantern, and some blankets. We stood and talked for a while. She told of her trip to America with her husband and two children.

"It was more than twenty years ago," she said, "Maybe closer to thirty. We crossed the stormy ocean in a small ship, a hard voyage. We landed in Philadelphia. We purchased a wagon and joined several German families in a great journey down the Great Wagon Road to this place in the wilderness. When we saw this place, we knew we wanted to spend the rest of our lives here. I think what we liked so much was the way the light struck the treetops in the morning, along with the sweet scents that surrounded these hills.

"We lost our son soon after we settled here. His name was Johann. It broke our hearts. But soon we were blessed with a beautiful baby girl who we named Ursula. And Gretchen, the daughter that made the journey with us grew up and become a fine woman. She is the mother of the children that you played with today. I hope you understand why she did not come out today."

"Of course," I said.

When Klaus and Ursula came in, they were holding hands and smiling. I knew that Klaus was going to cause big trouble.

That night, after Frau Becker and Ursula had bid us good night and returned to the cabin, Klaus told me he was not leaving with the regiment. He intended to remain in

North Carolina with Ursula and her family. I didn't argue very much. He knew the risk. The penalty for desertion in the time of war is death. He said he didn't care.

Albert appeared at sunrise the next morning. He said that the regiment was moving out, marching to Hillsborough. Nathanael Greene and his army had crossed over into Virginia, and General Cornwallis had decided not to chase them any more. We were going to make our camp in Hillsborough and wait.

Albert was not surprised to hear that Klaus planned to stay. We both wished our friend well. Albert and I agreed to take Klaus' musket and knapsack back with us. We would report that Klaus was shot in the back by a rebel sniper. We were sure that our story would be believed because that sort of thing was happening more often than ever. We embraced our friend for the last time. Klaus and Ursula stood watching as we waved and trudged off though forest. We never saw our comrade again.

Gretchen

My name is Gretchen Metzinger. I live in North Carolina with my husband and my three children. We live with my mother, my sister, her husband, and my lovely little niece. My husband returned from the war a few months ago. He fought with General George Washington. They defeated General Cornwallis and the British army at Yorktown up in Virginia. North Carolina and the other twelve colonies have formed a new nation we call the United States of America.

We are building a new cabin for Ursula and Klaus, my sister and her husband. Klaus was a British soldier who deserted from his army to stay with Ursula and become her husband. He was from Hesse, in Germany. The British hired soldiers from other countries because they didn't have enough young men in their own country to govern the vast British Empire. Klaus and many of his countrymen joined the British army for the chance to travel, for the excitement,

27

and for the money.

On the day that he and his friends marched on to our farm and intruded in our lives, my mother greeted them as if they were old friends. I was furious with her. My husband, Will, was a soldier in General Washington's colonial army. These men were the enemy. They appeared on the crest of the hill clutching little Daniel's arm as if he were a prisoner. Mama invited them for a meal in the yard and fed them as if they were honored guests.

Though I didn't agree with her, I understand the reason for her actions. She was happy to be among Germans again, to be speaking German. Klaus was one of the six soldiers that emerged from the woods that day. He never left. He bid his friends goodbye and stayed to become Ursula's husband.

Klaus and Ursula took the wagon to Salem, a Moravian town two days' ride to the west. The Moravians are a German religious group that came to North Carolina many years ago from Pennsylvania. They traveled down the Great Wagon Road, just as we did when I was a baby. The Moravians purchased a large tract of land and built Salem and two other towns. They called their land Wachovia. Klaus and Ursula got married and spent their wedding night in the inn at Salem.

Klaus has turned out to be a wonderful husband. He's been a big help on the farm. He's a very hard worker, and he knows a lot about farming. He and Will are preparing the land for planting. Klaus is also an excellent carpenter, like my husband Will. And he's a fair blacksmith. Daniel, Helga, and Joshua all love him. He spends a lot of time with them. Klaus and Ursula have a baby girl of their own, and they want to have many more children. I'm sure that they'll be good parents. We do not know what became of Klaus' fellow soldiers. After they left him here, their regiment marched to Hillsborough and stayed there until General Nathanael Greene and the North Carolina patriots engaged them in a fierce battle. They met at Guilford Courthouse, not far from here. It was North

Carolina's most ferocious battle of the American Revolution. The British lost so many men in that battle that they could not continue their campaign. Cornwallis marched his army down to Wilmington, desperately in need of supplies and reinforcements. After two weeks' rest, they set out on a long march north to a place in Virginia named Yorktown. I am telling all this because Yorktown is where George Washington and my husband Will trapped the British and defeated them to end the war. Will said that they could not have done it without the help of the French navy.

That was in October, 1781. Will made it home in time for Christmas. They had parades and celebrations in towns all over North Carolina to welcome the boys home and to celebrate our freedom as a new nation.

Klaus has not heard any news from his friends yet. He wrote his mother four months ago and invited her to come to North Carolina to live. We hope he receives a reply soon, but the mail does not come to our community very often. When it does, it is always several months old. Especially mail from Europe. It's wonderful to have the family together again. Our life here in the backcountry is hard, but we're happy here. I still think about my father, my older brother Johann, and the two little ones that we lost to the fever before Ursula came, but I try not to dwell on it for long. It will not bring them back to us. I just try to enjoy each day with the loved ones who are with us.

BOBBY WIESNER

Sweat crept down my neck in spite of the breeze that swept through the harbor. I spotted my ship, the *USS Chicago*, a half mile away, one of the many Navy warships that lined the sides of the pier and loomed above me like the walls of some mountain canyon.

My suitcase had not seemed heavy when I lifted it from my bed the night before, but during the thirty-minute walk from the main gate, my clean underwear from home had turned to bricks, and I had switched hands several times.

The journey from back home had taken all day. It had been good to see Mama and Pa and my brothers and little sister again, but ten days in rural eastern North Carolina was about a week too long. In 1968 southern California was a hectic, irreverent place at an outrageous moment in history. I was glad to be back.

I stopped to watch the sailboats in the harbor, tiny white shapes on a lake of color, close enough to touch. I took a deep breath, picked up the bag, squared my shoulders, and continued.

The giant cranes in the distance were still, as were the trucks and trams that roared down the pier on workdays. No sailors, suspended from the main decks, chipped away at the copious layers of paint on the great gray hulls. Also missing were the civilian workers in blue jeans and work shoes, smoking and drinking soft drinks and laughing beneath raised welding helmets, probably at us taxpayers who paid their salaries. It was Sunday. Only a trace of the smell of oil and paint and smoke lingered in the salt air.

The young marine on guard duty snapped to attention as I approached the steps that led to the ship's brow. He didn't salute. I was in civies. I climbed the steps and lugged my suitcase across the narrow wooden walkway to the ship's main deck. The tide was in, and the steep climb to the deck of the ship was not an easy one. I paused at the halfway point and came to attention, facing the flag at the ship's stern. Then I turned to face the Officer of the Watch.

"Permission to come aboard, sir."

"Permission granted."

The officer on the quarterdeck gave me an exaggerated salute and a broad smile. It was my good friend, Lieutenant junior grade Michael Burkhardt. Mike had been on duty when I reported aboard for the first time almost exactly one year before. I'll never forget that day. I am six-two, and when I stood at attention before him, his face and all that loomed above his Adam's apple were hidden by the visor on my cap. He would have been an imposing figure, standing there in his spotless white uniform, but for his perpetual grin. He looked as if he had just heard a good joke and was planning to retell it.

"Welcome back, Lieutenant j.g. Faulkner," he said as he offered his baseball glove-size hand.

"What are you talkin' about, Mike?"

"You made j.g. You and Maglio. Congratulations."

"Thanks."

I was no longer a lowly ensign. We were at the height of the Vietnam War, and the Navy had reduced the time to make j.g. from eighteen months to one year.

We shook hands. The energy in his grasp and his amicable disposition were contagious. Just being around him made me feel good. One of the most intelligent officers on the ship, Mike was one of a growing number of members of the crew, including me, that had doubts about whether the ship's mission was worthwhile.

"We have a departure date. Twenty-two August. Three weeks from tomorrow."

"So soon? Hellfire, we just got back from the last cruise," I said.

"I know. Deployed nine months, back home for four. Some of the married guys are sick about it."

We peered absently at the destroyer across the pier framed by the cloudless California sky.

"So, did you enjoy yourself down in shit-kicking country?" asked Burkhardt.

"Probably about as exciting as Scranton, Pennsylvania." Scranton was Burkhardt's home.

"Dull, huh?" Burkhardt grinned.

"I feel lucky to be back," I told him. "That was the worse flight I've ever had. We went through the thunderstorm to beat all thunderstorms. The lights went out. We fell hundreds of feet, several times. I thought the plane was comin' apart. After we finally flew out of it, the sky turned bright red."

"Sounds like one of the amusement park rides back home," he said.

"Anybody here that's going ashore tonight? Maglio or Wiesner around?"

"Who?"

"Maglio?"

"He's over at the O' club, buying drinks. He said to tell you he picked up a set of silver bars for you when he bought his."

"How about Bobby?"

"I know I'm about to step into some shit that passes for humor down in Hee-haw Land, but I'll bite. Who the hell is Bobby?"

"Bobby Wiesner, your sweetheart."

"Don't listen to him, Davis," Burkhardt chuckled. "He's just angry about the way women flock to me when we go out on the town. Like the young English lass we met downtown the night before he went on leave."

The young seaman who was standing watch with Burkhardt flashed a perplexed grin. Davis was a short, slender figure with pale blue eyes. When he smiled, his thin lips almost disappeared.

"Davis, has Mr. Wiesner left the ship during this watch?" I asked.

Davis continued his lifeless grin. "When I was on the *Pratt* we had a Mr. Wiseman," he said, unsure of whether we were pulling his leg.

"Okay, Burkhardt, you did a good job of coachin' young Davis here. You boys been practicin' all day?"

Then I saw the look in Mike's eyes, and I knew something was terribly wrong. He was not kidding around. He studied my face carefully. The expression on my face must have conveyed the message that I was serious, also. I didn't know what to say.

"I'm goin' down below." I said.

"I'll see you at dinner."

"Okay, Mike."

On the deck below, I stepped into the ward room, a space large enough to seat one hundred officers at meal time as well as provide them with a place to relax. Four officers were playing bridge and another was watching television. All looked up and greeted me half-heartedly as I hurried through with my bag of bricks.

I deposited my load in the stateroom that Maglio and I shared and backtracked two doors to Wiesner's room. I gripped the knob with a sweaty hand, turned it and pushed the door open far enough to get my head inside. My pulse raced. A young communications officer slept innocently in the top bunk, the one that Bobby Wiesner had occupied for the past year.

I closed the door and hurried forward to the junior officers' bunkroom, ducking as I stepped through each of the watertight doorways. In the bunkroom were two new ensigns that had come aboard during my absence. None of the other officers were around. I introduced myself quickly and returned to my stateroom. I needed to shower and change and figure out what to do next.

I showered quickly. Amazingly, hot water was available. I slipped into a clean set of whites and headed aft to the crew's quarters. OI Division living spaces were on the second deck, near the stern. Wiesner had been the OI Division Officer before I inherited it.

I stopped Petty Officer Second Class Vick as he emerged from the division's near-deserted sleeping quarters. He was on his way to relieve the watch.

"Vick."

"Oh, Mr. Faulkner. Welcome back. Did you hear about the Chief? He got orders to the Great Lakes."

"No, I just got here a few minutes ago. Say, Vick... This may sound strange, but I'm lookin' for Mr. Wiesner, and some of the crew members acted real strange when I asked about him."

"Who?" Vick wore an expression similar to Burkhardt's. "Mr. Faulkner..."

"Let me guess. You never heard of a Wiesner."

"That's right, Sir."

"Vick, Lieutenant j.g. Wiesner was your division officer all last cruise."

"I beg your pardon, Sir. Mr. White was our division officer until he got discharged. Then you took over. I never heard of anyone named Wiesner."

I didn't answer. We looked at one another for several seconds.

"I gotta go topside and relieve the watch, Sir."

"Okay, Vick. I didn't mean to hold you up."

"You gonna be okay?"

"Sure. I just...I don't know. I guess... I just don't know."

"Sorry I couldn't help you. See you later, Mr. Faulkner."

Back in the wardroom the officers discussed the departure date for the upcoming cruise. Some of the wives were arriving for the evening meal. I went back down to Bobby's stateroom. The door opened and the communications officer emerged, headed for the wardroom. His short dark hair stood straight up. "Hiya, Faulkner," he said, with a smile.

I mumbled a greeting and continued down the narrow passageway. What was I going to say? I wanted to look for my friend in your stateroom. You don't know him. He's my imaginary friend.

I climbed the five flights of steps that led to the bridge. The wheel, the engine order telegraph, and the gyro compass waited patiently in silence. I stepped up and took a seat in the brown leather captain's chair on the starboard side. I pulled a Winston from the pack in my shirt pocket and lit it, hardly noticing the postcard panorama of the harbor before me.

I was stunned. Numb. I stumbled, sleepwalking, in the middle of some weird dream. Maybe the taxi had deposited me on the set of the *Twilight Zone*. I was ready for Rod Sterling to take the stage and wrap this episode up. I knew that there was an officer on the ship named Bobby Wiesner. Why did everyone else deny his existence? He had been a veteran of the previous cruise when I joined the ship a year ago. I was just out of Officer Candidate School. Boy, was I green. I was assigned to the Operations Department, and old Bobby had guided me though the learning process necessary for me to become a CIC Watch Officer.

Bobby was a bright, very knowledgeable, and somewhat cynical individual. He had a good sense of humor, but he kept to himself, and because he was quiet, thoughtful, maybe even aloof, he was not the most popular junior officer on the ship. We were the same age, twenty-four, but Bobby seemed older.

It must have been this quiet confidence that women found irresistible. He was over six feet, slim, upright. His hair was coal-black, and he had a long nose with slightly flaring nostrils and dark eyes that shone after he'd had several drinks. He was an agile dancer, and he attracted the most beautiful women whether the nightclub was in Los Angeles, Honolulu, or Hong Kong. He was the only person I knew besides my uncle who still smoked non-filter cigarettes.

He came from Buffalo, from a working-class family. His mother was a public school teacher. He graduated from Syracuse University, and his younger brother was a student there. The brother and his friends back home were giving Bobby a hard time about being in the military. The anti-war movement was picking up steam, especially on the campuses.

I slid from my perch and made my way to the door of the Combat Information Center, my principal workplace when we were underway. I pushed open the door and entered the cold, dark cavern of red and green indicator lights and the incessant drone of the air conditioner. I could see Wiesner standing there with his impish grin, waiting for me to relieve him from the watch. Now several radar repeaters and other pieces of equipment lay open, their wiring hanging, works in progress. I pulled out another cigarette and lit it.

I decided to go back below and find Burkhardt. He had been relieved from duty and I caught up with him in the wardroom. We went forward to his stateroom. He pulled two Cokes from his tiny refrigerator and handed one to me.

"I heard it costs ten thousand dollars for us to fire one round. We fired thirty-five hundred times in one week during the Tet Offensive," Burkhardt was saying.

"Maybe we should drop dollars instead of bombs. It would be cheaper," I said. Bobby Wiesner had once said that.

We sat and sipped in silence.

36

"No offense, Lou, man, but you don't look too good. You okay?"

"I really don't know, Mike. First I fly across the country through a storm so bad everybody on board pees in their pants. Then when I finally get here one of my best friends is missing, and nobody ever heard of him. Either I'm crazy or you guys hatched up the practical joke of the century or somethin' real weird is goin' on here."

"I didn't want to bring it back up. I'm just glad it's this Bobby that's missing and not me."

"Very funny. Look, Mike, this thing has me goin'. Help me out here."

"I'm sorry man. Look, let's check out the cruise book. It hit the streets while you were gone."

He took the book from a shelf above his desk. It looked like a high school yearbook. I opened it and smelled the ink, flipping to the pictures of the officers. No Wiesner. He handed me the book from the previous cruise. Once again, no Wiesner. I turned to OI Division. No Wiesner. Lieutenant j.g. White was the division officer. Suddenly I felt cold, very heavy. My arms, my legs weighed a ton.

"What d'ya think, Louis? Any answers?"

I didn't answer. I couldn't.

"You don't look too good, Louis. Lie down here on my bunk for a while."

I did as he suggested. I slept for almost an hour. When I woke up, I cleaned up and decided to go over to the officer's club to find Maglio.

I went to the wardroom to find Burkhardt. He and the rest of the duty section were required to remain on board for the full twenty-four hours. They were about to be served the evening meal.

"You're going to miss a great flick tonight. An early Bogart." Even as he grinned, he studied me, searching my face for signs of lunacy.

"I need to get away for a few minutes. I'll see you later."

The officer's club was crowded. Maglio had had

more than his share of the inexpensive drinks served there. When he saw me he pounded me on the back and ordered a Scotch for me. It was still early when I returned to the ship that evening. Several of the other junior officers helped me carry Maglio aboard.

The next morning I went about my duties as if Bobby Wiesner had never existed. Weeks passed, and the day of our departure arrived. Spouses, families, and girl friends stood on the pier and bid us a tearful goodbye as the lines were cast off and the great ship slipped out to the channel and moved slowly through the harbor. Three weeks later we arrived at our station off the coast of Vietnam. There we steamed along the beach and fired our big guns at real and imagined targets called in by the Marines in the jungle. Burkhardt and I never mentioned the subject of Bobby Wiesner again though we stayed in touch until he died of cancer in 1989. I never told Maglio or any of the others. Over the years I came to accept it and to empathize with those who have sighted UFO's and those who have had brain tumors to miraculously disappear. I told my brothers, and I told my wife and my children, and we all spent time speculating and attempting to unravel the mystery. It was almost forgotten for many years until 1999, when a new piece of the puzzle fell into place.

In 1990 my wife and I drove to Norfolk for our first annual reunion of the crew of the *USS Chicago*. Thereafter we attended the event each year. We looked forward to our October trips to Philadelphia, Charleston, St. Louis, Seattle, or Los Angeles. In 1999 the crew met in Boston.

Each year the numbers of the World War II veterans decreased as they passed into the next world, but the number of Vietnam veterans increased as each year the faces of those who just got the word about the reunions appeared. One such newcomer was Nat Pond, formerly Quartermaster Second Class Pond. Nat lived in Cleveland. He had served on board from 1966 through 1968, and he and I had had several long conversations during those long watches on the bridge while crossing the Pacific. In those days, Pond had been tall and slim, with sandy blond hair. Now he was gray and bald and several pounds overweight, like me. He and his wife were quickly welcomed to our growing circle of Vietnam veterans.

It was late afternoon of the second day of the reunion that I looked in Nat's cruise book. Four or five of us gathered to relive our experiences of long ago and to enjoy each others' company along with a keg of cold beer. Many of us had brought our cruise books, pictures, and souvenirs to share with the group. I had left my cruise books in my hotel room, so I borrowed Nat's to put a face with a name someone had mentioned. When I opened it, I saw a large picture of Bobby Wiesner, along with several other members of the crew, studying a chart on the table in the Combat Information Center. I turned to the officers' photos, and there he was, Robert A. Wiesner, very much alive. Once again I went cold, and my limbs became very heavy.

"Excuse me," I said. I stood and made my way to the door.

"You okay, Louis?" It was Maglio.

"I'll be right back. Goin' to the can."

He didn't believe me. He followed me to the head and watched as I deposited several cups of beer and the mixture of peanuts and pretzels that I had consumed that afternoon, into the toilet.

"You never could hold your liquor," he said.

"I was always the one that poured your ass in a cab and dragged you back on board," I told him as I wiped my face with a wet towel.

He followed me to the elevator and delivered me to my wife who we woke from her nap. When we were alone, I told her.

"I saw Bobby Wiesner. His picture. In a cruise book. Nat Pond's cruise book."

She sank to the bed beside me. "You mean the one who..."

"Yep. After all these years."

"Are you okay? You look like shit."

"Thanks. Look Sally, put on your clothes and go down and bring Nat up here. Tell him to bring his book. Please."

She did as I asked, and fifteen minutes later the three of us sat around the little table next to the window.

"What's this all about, Louis? Sally said it was an emergency."

I opened his book and pointed. "Nat, do you remember this man? Bobby Wiesner?"

"Sure I do. I used to stand watches with him. What about him?"

"Nat, when I returned to the ship after two weeks' leave in the summer of 1968, he was no longer on the ship. Not only that, but nobody remembered Bobby Wiesner bein' on the ship at all. In fact, his picture was not in the cruise books. It was as if he'd never existed."

"What do you mean?"

"Exactly what I said. Here, take a look at my book. He's not there."

The three of us sat and compared the books. They were almost identical, but a few pages were different.

"Louis, have you asked around downstairs? Lets find out if anyone else remembers Mr. Wiesner."

"I asked three people the day I came back. They all looked at me as if I were a lunatic. I thought I was, too. Until now. Where were you that day? And did you notice that he was gone?"

Nat thought about it. "I was discharged in 1968. He was on board when I left, I think."

"What was the date?"

"July 31 was my last day. I caught a flight to Detroit on the first of August."

"Did you have your cruise book with you?"

"Yes. In fact, I believe it came out just a few days before I left the ship."

We sat there, processing the new information, trying to make sense of it all and to solve a thirty-year-old mystery.

"What do you and me and this book have in common that no one else shares?" I asked.

We thought some more.

"What day did you arrive back from leave?" Nat asked.

"August first. The day after you left. Whatever happened, happened that night."

"I'll never forget that fight home," Nat said. "We went through the worse thunderstorm I ever saw. The lights went out. We fell hundreds of feet, several times. After we finally flew out of it, the sky turned bright red."

We didn't solve the puzzle that weekend, but Nat and I have become best e-mail buddies, and we discuss it once in a while. This sounds weird, but we believe that the storm we went through that day knocked us out of our time strand and into another. We left the strand where Bobby had joined the Navy and been assigned to the *Chicago*. We landed in one where either Bobby had not been born or had not joined the Navy. Or if he did, he'd been assigned to some other ship. One day Nat and I will meet in Buffalo and try to look old Bobby up.

At least Sally doesn't think I'm crazy any more.

JAMES CITY

Life on the Farm

My name is James Corbett. I was a slave until three years ago. I had spent my whole life working on the farm of Mr. Frank Corbett of Jones County in North Carolina. I lived there with Mama and my two sisters, Rose and Florence. I never knew my daddy. Mama said he was sold when I was a baby. My brother Jesse and, before him, another brother, Willie, were also sold. Mama said Mr. Corbett had to keep selling his slaves to keep from going broke. His farm was not a very big one and he was not what you would call a real good farmer.

Anyhow, Mama had been saying for as long as I can remember that she was not going to lose any more of her children by having them sold because we were going to run away. I never paid her much mind, though. Old Reverend Luther Collins, who lived down the road on the Ferguson place, told me before he died that they didn't have slavery "up north." I didn't know where up north was. He said it was places like New York, Pennsylvania, and

Massachusetts. He said the white folks up there didn't believe in slavery and there were black folks living up there who were free. I didn't know what free meant, but it sounded real good.

"But it takes three or four weeks, maybe more, to get up north," Reverend Collins said, "and then the slave catchers could come and get you even after you got up there. Why, I knew a slave boy once by the name of Daniel who ran," he said. "Daniel hid in the woods durin' the day and walked all night long every night for three weeks and got to Virginia. Then he got caught and brought back. His master kept him locked in the corn crib for a week, and then he sold him to a slave trader bound for Mississippi."

So as bad as Mama might want to up and escape, we knew that it was something that was just about impossible. But then the war started and a lot of the white men around went off to join the Confederate army to fight the Yankees. They said it started at Fort Sumter, down in Charleston, South Carolina. Then I started hearing about how the Yankees were coming down to North Carolina to free us slaves. We talked about the Yankees a lot and looked down the road in hopes that they were coming. Well, they didn't come, so we kind of gave up on them.

Now let me tell how it was on the farm. I liked working on the farm. I did all the plowing and planting and feeding the hogs and milking the cow. Mama and Florence did the cooking. Mr. and Mrs. Corbett were getting old and their daughters had both gotten married and moved away.

Now, in a way, Mr. Corbett was not a bad master. He never raised his voice at us and he always fed us good and made sure we had warm clothes. And he let us plant our own garden and keep chickens. And he let me keep my own sow, as long as I gave him a pig from each litter.

In return, we tried to do a good job on the farm. I didn't slow down real slow when he was gone, or play sick, or break the man's tools like some slaves on other farms did. I always figured if I did a real good job for my master he would think he couldn't do without me, and he wouldn't sell me.

That was what we were all afraid of those days, being sold to one of those big plantation owners down in Mississippi or Georgia. They say that those plantations might have a hundred slaves or more and that the owners just don't care about their slaves. Poor food, chains, whipping, and ignorant overseers were what you had to look forward to if you got sold to them. So I made sure I worked hard and that Mr. Corbett was happy with my work. Mrs. Corbett was old and sickly, and Mama and Florence and Rose took real good care of her. We were the only four slaves the Corbetts had, so I figured we were safe as long as one of them didn't die.

Of course, there were some things I didn't like. First of all, Mr. Corbett thought he was always right and that I was too ignorant to be making suggestions. For example, I told him that I heard that most farmers had started leaving some land out and not planting it for one year. And that they tried to plant something different in each field from what they had planted the year before. But he went right on with cotton in the back field, corn beside the house, and tobacco across the road, every year. And it seemed like the harvest was getting smaller and smaller each year.

The other thing I didn't like was the way Mr. Corbett acted when he was around other white people. They would talk about how ignorant we were and would tell stories about the stupid things that their slaves had done and laugh their old mean laugh. I knew Mr. Corbett didn't really feel that way about Mama and the girls and me, but I never heard him say one good word to them about us, and it hurt.

On the Run

Mama had been threatening to take us all and run for a long time, so when she came home late one afternoon in March, 1862, and told us that she heard that the Yankees had captured New Bern, she had to repeat it to get us to listen.

"I heard them talking in Trenton today," she said, clutching my arm. "The Yankees have taken over the whole town of New Bern and freed all the slaves, they said, and once the word got out, slaves from all over the countryside was runnin' to the Yankees."

Rose and I looked at one another. We couldn't believe it. I let out a howl and when Florence rushed in she found Rose and Mama and me dancing, hand-in-hand, in a circle. Mama started to cry, and she pulled all of us to her.

"We going to be free, children," she cried. This time, we believed her.

We made plans to make our escape the next week. Mama started putting up food for us to take with us. We planned to slip away late one night, walk till morning, and hide during the day. We figured it would take three days. We worried about wading through the swamps at night because it was the first week of April, almost time for snakes. But we wanted to be free mighty bad, more than we were afraid of snakes.

I felt bad about leaving Mr. Corbett at planting time. I even thought about staying until the crops were planted, but I knew we had better make our break while no one was expecting it. Besides, Mr. Corbett was going to be fit to be tied no matter when we lit out.

I was nervous all day on the day we planned to escape. I was afraid Mr. or Mrs. Corbett would find out and call the sheriff. I was breaking land behind old Pat, my favorite mule. I knew I would miss the mules and the cow. I had told them about all my troubles over the years. I would miss our cabin and the farm. After all, it had been my home all my life.

I put up the mule, fed all the livestock, and just before sundown I strolled over to our cabin, slow and easy, tied up in knots on the inside. Rose was inside, all to pieces. I hugged her. She was a tall, a little on the skinny side, not at all like Mama and Florence who were both short and stout. Rose took a deep breath and relaxed a little.

Her eyes lit up when a big smile flashed on her face. We waited for Mama and Florence to come back from the main house. They had to cook and serve supper to the Corbetts, wash the dishes, and put Mrs. Corbett to bed.

It was a little cool, so I started a small fire to take the chill off. When they came in, nobody said a word. Mama had brought some rice, a little chicken, and some biscuits for supper. After we had eaten, she and Florence wrapped the corn bread, sausage, boiled eggs, and biscuits in big handkerchiefs. Then we quietly pulled on our coats and crept out into the darkness. When we reached the road, we turned and looked back for the last time. When I glanced at the women, I could barely see their faces in the starlight, but I could see their teeth shining because they were all grinning, just like me.

We hid in the woods while it was light and sneaked along the roads at night. We never ran out of food, but I stole some meat from a smokehouse in a farmyard we passed, just in case. I had to kill the farmer's dog with a hoe handle when he got after me.

The next night, we heard a horse coming up behind us. We ducked into the woods and got real quiet. One of us stepped on some dry twigs that sounded almost like gunshots on such a still night. We all held our breath, knowing they were coming to take us back.

We expected to see the sheriff's men on fast horses, chasing bloodhounds. What we saw when he finally rounded the bend was a big old work horse just plodding along, pulling a wagon in the shadows of the trees. We could make out that the driver was a black man, and Mama and the girls gave out a big sigh. When the old wagon got closer, we could see the tops of several scarf-covered heads in the back, bouncing a little whenever they hit a bump. I whispered for the others to stay where they were, and I slipped off to catch up with the wagon.

"Where ya'll headed?" I called out from the darkness.

One of the women squealed once, sharp and quick.

46

The driver pulled on the reins and reached down to grab a shotgun and point it at me. His floppy hat fell to the ground and his hair shone white in the moonlight like a big old cotton boll.

"Hold on, now. I don't mean no harm."

"Step out and show yourself," the driver said. His voice sounded like he meant business.

"Put that gun away and I will."

"Who you got with you?"

"I'm by myself. I'm comin' out, now. Take it easy."

Four women and three children raised up enough to peep at me over the side of the wagon.

"Well, now, a whole wagon full. In the middle of the night, too. You people got to be slaves on the run."

"You leave us alone, mister. We ain't bothered you."

"Naw, all I'm saying is if you was slaves on the run, going to New Bern, I was going to ask you if I could come along. I'm in the same boat as you."

The old man let out a sigh and lowered his weapon.

"Climb on up, then. We need to move on out."

"Well, there's one thing I didn't tell you. I never ran before, and I figure a man on the run can't be too careful. I got my family hid back there in the woods."

"How many more you got?"

"There's four of us in all."

"Good God, where we goin' put 'em all?"

He glanced at the wagon as if he were placing the newcomers in their seats. He retrieved his hat and planted it on his shaggy head.

"Go get 'em," he said. "We'll squeeze you in one way or the other."

It was a tight fit, but they all acted like they were glad to have us. There was old man Isaac and his wife, three daughters, and his grandchildren, all from the Pierce plantation. Everybody was excited. We kept our voices low, but everyone chattered at one time. Especially that youngest daughter. Man, could she talk. She still can. We

47

have been together ever since that night. When I first saw her that night, talking Florence's ear off, I thought she was the most lively, most exciting woman I had ever met. I knew she was the one for me. When I finally got the chance to ask her her name, she said it was Jewel. What a lucky night it was for me.

Isaac said that he thought we should be near New Bern. He was right. At first light, we pulled off the road down a path to hide behind an old barn. I jumped off and ran back to brush away our tracks. While I was brushing, I heard what sounded like a herd of horses galloping toward us. When I saw them coming around the curve and realized who the riders were, I almost fell over. It was a whole bunch of soldiers in two straight rows. The second man was holding a pole with a United States flag flapping as they rode along, and every man in those long lines wore dark blue uniforms. They were Yankees. I normally would have jumped into a ditch and hid, but I stayed where I was. I wanted to be seen this time. When they got up close, I could see that they were going to ride right on by, so I ran out on the road and waved and shouted at them.

I thought they would stop, but they didn't. They rode right on by. I felt like a fool, standing there in the big cloud of dust they raised. But then two of them turned around and came back to talk to me.

"Are you an escaped slave?" one of them asked, in a voice that sounded kind of bored. I thought maybe he didn't like being left behind. It made me feel like that maybe he didn't feel like I was worth the trouble. Later I found out that I was wrong. That's just the way soldiers carry themselves. "I'm Corporal O'Malley. We were ordered to escort you back to our camp for ex-slaves."

"Well, I'll be," I heard myself say. "I got some more folks behind that barn, Mister Corporal. You wait right there, and I'll run and fetch 'em." I can tell you, I have never run so fast or hollered so loud. I could not believe it! We were free!

When the folks behind the barn heard me, they

48

came running out, crying, hugging me and hugging each other. The girls grabbed each other's hands and jumped up and down. Mama was bawling.

"What did I tell you!" she cried. "What did I tell you!"

New Bern

Well, that was three years ago. A lot has happened since then. When we got to New Bern that day the white folks there couldn't have treated us any better. They acted almost like they had been expecting us. First they took us into this big building and gave us something to eat. Then they had each one of us to sit in a chair, and they asked us our names, where we came from, our master's name, what kind of work we knew how to do, and several more questions. They told us they would find us a place to stay and give us all a job and pay us. I asked them how much they paid. They said eight dollars a month. We couldn't believe it. Nobody had ever paid us two cents for our work. Mama and the girls kept shaking their heads and brushing away tears. What a glorious day that was.

We had this little cabin to spend the night in, right next to where Isaac and his crowd were staying. They all came over and man, did we have a celebration out in the yard. Old man Isaac played his harmonica while the rest of us danced around a big fire. A few soldiers gathered around to watch us. They had a jug of whiskey, and they poured a cupful for Isaac and another one for me.

The next day the soldiers that had ridden by me the day before returned to New Bern, and they brought four more wagon loads of slaves with them and a bunch more walking. They were shouting and waving at us, and the soldiers seemed almost as happy as the slaves did. The soldiers called us "contrabands".

The driver of the last wagon was a tall dark man a few years older than me. He looked mighty familiar, and when he saw me, he almost fell down laughing. He was

George Harris from right up the road from our place, maybe four miles at the most. We had known each other all our lives.

The next day, some more slaves came, and the next day some more. I bet there were a hundred or more that came in just that week. One that came in from up above Kinston was Furney Bryant. He was this old big strong dumb-looking guy who was not dumb at all. He was smart. And he kept George and me laughing all the time. The three of us stuck together for the next three years.

New Bern was a beautiful town in the spring, at least it was that spring. Part of the town had been set afire by the Confederates when they got run out by the Yankees, but most of it looked just like there was no war going on at all. The leaves on the shade trees were coming out, and there were all kinds of colorful flowers everywhere.

They moved us into some houses that used to belong to white folks. The white folks had left in such a hurry that they had left a lot of clothes and pots and pans and other belongings behind. Our house was a white, one-story house on the corner with a nice-sized front porch. It was not anything fancy, but it was it was a lot bigger and nicer than our cabin on the Corbett place.

George and Furney and me all went to work down at the docks unloading supplies for the Union army. We felt good about what we were doing. We figured we were helping the soldiers that were fighting to free the slaves. Mama and Florence went to work cooking for the army. Rose worked in the laundry.

After work, we went to school to learn to read. The soldiers had set up a night school for us. Back then the teachers were mostly soldiers. A lot of them had been college professors and teachers up in Massachusetts. They acted like they sure enjoyed teaching us. There were about eight hundred of us in those first two schools. Learning to read was not as hard as I thought it would be. We also got to go to church all we wanted to. Some went to the African Methodist church and some went to a new black Baptist church. Later on, we started a new church that somebody named the African Methodist Episcopal Zion church. We got to know the man in charge of taking care of poor people, black and white, for the whole coast of North Carolina. His name was Mr. Vincent Colyer, a preacher. He was a fine man. We all thought the world of him. He got General Burnside to open a hospital in New Bern for us slaves. He even preached at our church a few times.

Jewel and I got married that fall. Those were some happy times. Christmas that year was the best one we had ever had or thought about having.

Then just when we thought things couldn't get any better, President Lincoln freed all the slaves with his Emancipation Proclamation. This meant an end to slavery. It meant that from then on all those Yankee soldiers were now fighting to free us slaves. We had the biggest celebration that New Bern had ever seen. There was dancing in the streets, a little parade, and a lot of drinking and singing and praying. Mama said, "See what I told you!"

That same month, Reverend Horace James was selected to be the new Superintendent of Negro Affairs. Boy, was he something. By 1863, we were bursting at the seams. A lot of people were sleeping in warehouses, and some in tents. It seemed like we were getting a hundred new contrabands every day. Well, Reverend James was determined to do something about it. He got some land on the other side of the Trent River and we went to work building a town for all the new contrabands to live in. We called it the Trent River camp. The logging crew kept dragging logs up to the camp, and our crew sawed them the right length, notched them out, and built a cabin for each family. We left plenty of space between cabins so the families could plant corn and other vegetables to eat. Before we were through we built a school, a hospital, a blacksmith shop, and two churches.

In the Army

I didn't stay to finish building the camp because George, Furney and me joined the army. Yep, when Colonel Wild came through, he said the Emancipation Proclamation had authorized the army to use freed slaves for soldiers, and he was looking for good men to join the Yankee army. Well, he sure came to the right place, because it seemed like half the black men in New Bern joined up. And man oh man, were we proud of those bright blue uniforms. We learned how to march and salute and how to pitch a tent and how to shoot and reload and shoot again. We all learned all those things, but nobody took to the army any better than Furney did. It wasn't long before he had made corporal, and then sergeant. He made us all feel proud. He opened the eyes of a lot of those white soldiers that were kind of doubtful about us.

Mama was crying when she saw me in the uniform. I had thought it was because she was so proud, but she said it was because she was so afraid. She tried to be brave, but, in spite of herself, she dampened my pride a little. Jewel might have felt the same way Mama did, but she didn't let me know it if she did. She knew how important it was to me and to the other men that joined.

Another good thing about the Emancipation Proclamation was that we didn't have to worry any more about the British coming over here and helping the rebels. I didn't know anything about all this until Corporal Emmerton, one of our teachers, explained it to us. He said that the factories in England were closing down because they couldn't get enough cotton. They had been buying it from cotton dealers in Georgia, Alabama, Mississippi, and Louisiana, but now that the war had started, the dealers couldn't ship it out of the country. President Lincoln had ordered the United States Navy to blockade all Confederate seaports. He wanted to stop all shipping going in or out. The British government was thinking about stepping in to stop the fighting and get the cotton trade moving again. If they had and if the two sides had agreed to a truce, the country would have remained split apart forever. But now that Lincoln had freed the slaves, Corporal Emmerton said, the purpose of the war had changed some. A lot of people were saying now that the war was about making the South actually free the slaves. Corporal Emmerton said that the British would not dare come in and help the slave owners. The British hated slavery, he said. They had done away with it long ago. Everybody talked about how smart President Lincoln was.

We left New Bern in July, 1863. We marched proudly down the street before a large crowd that had turned out to see us off. They called us the Africa Brigade. We had our own banner. We marched all the way to Charleston, South Carolina. It was the first time most of us had ever set foot outside of North Carolina.

We pitched our tents at a place called Folly Island to wait for them to call us to go and fight. They never did call for us. They said General Gillmore had attacked Fort Wagner, but we had lost. We were disappointed that we didn't see any action, but we sure were glad when they told us we were leaving. It sure was hot down there. They loaded us on some ships, and we took our first ride out to sea. They took us to Norfolk, Virginia.

On the way, a storm came up and the seas got so rough that most of us got seasick. We were sure glad to see Norfolk. But then when we got off the ship we didn't get a chance to see the town. They sent us marching down south that same day. We spent the night in a big barn on a big plantation. Some of the boys stayed in the slave quarters.

We marched until we crossed over into North Carolina, and we kept on marching. Everywhere we went we started attracting big crowds of slaves, cheering as we marched by or just trying to get close enough to touch us. It made us feel mighty proud. We told them about how we were freed by the Yankees down in New Bern and now we were here to free them.

Furney had made sergeant down in Charleston. We were proud to serve under him. He had such a way about him in his sergeant's stripes, he was a big hit with the slaves.

When we got to this big swamp, we marched right on into it, with General Wild riding up ahead of us. It took us several days to get through the swamp. Then we got to Elizabeth City. When we marched in, we sent the white folks into a panic. They thought it was terrible that the Yankees were using black soldiers. We stayed there for seven days. Every day we went out on a raid. Sometimes we waited until that night. We were looking for these gangs of Confederate guerrillas. They had been attacking the Yankees stationed in the area, and we were there to put an end to it. Every time we went out on a raid, we brought back slaves who had joined up with us.

One night we came up on a Confederate guerilla camp out in the woods. They were all sitting around the fire, and we just surrounded them and hollered for them to put up their hands. We took all their horses and guns and ammunition and made them all march back to Elizabeth City. We had just left their camp when we heard a shot and Lieutenant Mann fell over, shot through the heart. The boys caught the sniper almost as soon as he had shot, and they beat him pretty bad. He had been on guard duty for the Confederates, but he had fallen asleep. When he woke up, he shot and killed the lieutenant. The sniper's name was Daniel Bright. When we got back to Elizabeth City, General Wild held a trial and ordered him hung.

When we left Elizabeth City, General Wild divided us into three detachments. Our platoon was placed under the command of Colonel Draper. We marched to Roanoke Island, and on the way we ran across three more Confederate guerilla camps. At one of the camps, we got into a big fight, and I killed three Confederates. One of them was just a boy. I felt real bad about it for a long time.

When we got to Roanoke Island, we were welcomed by the Yankees stationed there. We brought

54

over two thousand more freed slaves with us. Lieutenant Poole, one of the officers stationed there, told us that Roanoke Island was where the very first white people came and lived in the United States. He said they disappeared. Nobody knows if the Indians carried them off or if they marched off somewhere looking for something to eat or what. Anyhow, there were over a hundred people, men, women, and children, and nobody ever found hide nor hair of them. That's why they call it the Lost Colony.

Back in New Bern

When we marched in to New Bern that winter, a big crowd gave us a warm welcome, cheering and marching along beside us. All the officers reported that we had done a commendable job, for green troops. A newspaper had been started by some of the Massachusetts men, and they had a big article about our expedition. I was sure glad to see Jewel and Mama and the girls.

We spent the next few weeks helping to build fortifications around New Bern along the Neuse and the Trent Rivers. Most of it had already been done when we got there. We were sure glad we had because of what happened on the night of January 30.

The Battle of New Bern

It was after midnight and Jewel was shaking me. I wanted her to leave me alone. And somebody was beating on the door.

"James! ... James! ... It's me, George! Get up! We got to move out! The rebels is here! They done surrounded the town!"

Jewel swung the door open, and a cold wind made the fire flame up before George could get inside and shut the door.

"We got to hurry, James. Somebody said they crossed Bachelor's Creek and is gettin' ready to cross the

Trent River at Brice's Creek."

"Oh, my lord!" Jewel's eyes were big as two Yankee silver dollars. I knew what she was thinking. There were all kinds of stories about how the Confederates would hang black soldiers when they took them prisoner.

I got into my uniform, boots, and coat in a hurry.

"I got to wake up the rest of the boys. There'll be some wagons here for us in a few minutes," George said as he hurried back out.

Mama and the girls came in wanting to know what was going on, and Jewel was getting them all upset. Rose was starting to wail.

"Look, y'all," I said, "Hush that foolishness. There ain't no way no Johnny Reb is goin' to set foot in this town. We got the whole town protected by big banks of dirt and more cannons than you can count. You know because you've all seen 'em. And there is no tellin' how many soldiers there are in this town. Maybe ten thousand or more. So hush up so I can get on out of here and help out."

They quietened down after I said that. I took down my musket, my powder horn, my ammunition pouch, and my canteen. Jewel helped me get my knapsack on. She had packed me some sweet potatoes and cornbread and a piece or two of fried fatback. Each one of them gave me a kiss before I went out.

"Take care of yourself, honey," said Jewel.

"Goodbye, son," Mama said. "Trust in the Lord to keep you safe."

"Be careful, James," said Rose.

"You all go and lay back down," I said. "We're going to run those rebels off, and I'll be back before you know it."

The wagons were moving through the street, and the soldiers, black and white, were running from all different directions to jump on. Our wagon went to the fortification at Brice's Creek, where the Africa Brigade had been sent. We were in place before first light. You wouldn't be able to tell much until then.

"I heard the rebs were sendin' gunboats down the Neuse River," somebody said.

"They must mean business."

"I tell you one thing. They goin' have to shoot me dead. They won't take this old boy prisoner."

I think we all felt that way. There were a lot of stories about what the rebels did to black soldiers they captured.

The first cannon fire started about eight o'clock. I thought that first cannon ball that exploded against our outside wall was going to bust my eardrums. And then our guns, when they started to shoot back, were just as loud. All we did all day was sit there in the rain and wait for something else to happen. Nothing did. We had to sit and listen to all that noise all day long and all night long. I tell you my nerves were all to pieces. I think everyone else was the same way. Finally, sometime that next morning, the shooting stopped. We waited the rest of the day for the rebels to start across the river, but they never did. Then we heard that they had given up and were hightailing it back to Kinston through the swamps. You could hear a cheer going up all over. We had to stay there another night, just to make sure, but we really did not mind.

Later on we found out that the Confederates had attacked in three places. They had been led by a famous general, General Pickett. His army had gotten across Bachelor's Creek and was waiting for the other two detachments to reach New Bern, but our cannon fire from Fort Anderson on the Neuse River and from our fortifications on Brice's Creek had run them off. Finally, General Pickett just turned his men around and marched on back to Kinston.

The rebels had sent gunboats down the Neuse. They captured a Yankee gunboat named the *Underwriter*. A bunch of Confederate guerillas had come up from Wilmington and captured our barracks at Newport. Newport is a little town about twenty miles from New Bern on the road to Morehead City. They burned down the barracks, the storehouse, the stables, and the railroad bridge. Out in the country around New Bern, the rebels had destroyed homes and storehouses and carried off livestock and equipment. The worse news was that the enemy had captured over three hundred prisoners. Some of them were white boys from North Carolina that had deserted the Confederate army and joined up with us. Three weeks later Corporal Emmerton told us he heard that the Confederates had hung all twenty-two of those boys over in Kinston.

After that raid, General Peck ordered that all the contraband camps be consolidated into the one inside the fortifications, the Trent River settlement. We went to work building more cabins. Before we were done we had built almost eight hundred cabins.

Yellow Fever

That summer Florence and Rose both got married. Florence married William Long, a woodsman, and Rose married a farmer named John Bryan. They all seemed real happy. Our first child was due to be born around the first of October.

We should have known things were going along too good. We had some real bad luck that fall. A plague of Yellow Fever came to New Bern and it seemed like half the people in town got sick. Jewel got sick and lost the baby, but she got well. Mama was not that lucky. We lost her and we lost Rose and we lost one of Jewel's sisters. One of them would have been bad enough, but all of them at one time tore me apart. I tried to be strong, though, for Jewel and for Florence. Rose's new husband, John, was so hurt that he went off after the funeral and stayed in the woods by himself for almost two weeks.

The plague lasted two months. During that time people closed up their shops and stayed closed up inside their homes. Pitch and tar fires were burning out in the streets to purify the air. A cloud of smoke was hanging over the whole town. The coffin factory could not keep up with the orders. Hearses patrolled the streets to pick up the dead bodies. Somebody said we lost more than a thousand people.

Christmas that year was a sad time. And we didn't celebrate New Year's Day at all. But we knew we would somehow find the strength to carry on.

The End of the War

After the first of the year, the big news around town was about the attack on Wilmington and about the march of General William T. Sherman. Corporal Emmerton said that our army had finally captured Wilmington in January. We had been trying for three years to take it because Wilmington was a seaport where these special ships called blockade runners were sneaking in with supplies for General Robert E. Lee and his Confederate army. They said the supplies were shipped on the train from Wilmington to the army in Virginia. The capture of Wilmington was good news for our side.

The other big news was about General Sherman. He was a Yankee general who was marching his army across the South, burning houses and barns and stealing people's food and livestock. They had burned down almost the whole city of Atlanta, and then they marched all the way to Savannah. In February they were marching through the swamps of South Carolina, headed our way. I heard they freed slaves everywhere they went. Corporal Emmerton said they had 60,000 men with 2,500 wagons. He said the column was twenty-five miles long. They were living off the land as they marched.

General Sherman got to North Carolina in March, and there were two battles. One was at Averasboro and the biggest one was at Bentonville. I don't know where these places are, but I think they are out in the country somewhere around Fayetteville. Anyway, we won both of these battles, and everybody was saying that the war was

59

just about over.

They were right. General Lee surrendered to General Grant at Appomattox Courthouse up in Virginia in April, 1865. The war was finally over, and we were free forever! There was a lot of celebrating that night. I sure wished Mama and Rose could have been there to see it.

It meant that the fighting and the dying was over. The soldiers would be able to go home to their families. The Confederate soldiers and others who had left New Bern would be coming back.

Right behind the good news came the worst news of all. We heard that President Abraham Lincoln was dead. He had been shot to death. Corporal Emmerton said he had been shot while he was at a theatre, watching a play. A man named John Wilkes Booth had shot him because he was mad because President Lincoln had freed the slaves. It was a sad time around New Bern. I saw some of the toughest soldiers, white and black, crying. Corporal Emmerton said the whole nation was in mourning.

What, now?

What are we going to do with ourselves, now? A lot of people said that they are going to stay right where they are in James City. The Freedmen's Bureau had decided to change the name of the Trent River settlement to "James City", after Reverend Horace James, who started it. It couldn't have been named for a better man.

It is a good place, but Jewel and me are country folks. We have another baby on the way, now, and we hope to have several more. We may just go back to Jones County and see if old man Corbett needs somebody to farm his land for him. We could be sharecroppers. We'll offer to farm his land for him for half the crop in the fall. Jewel could cook for them, but they'll have to pay her. I wonder if he's still got my favorite mule, old Pat.

ONE SUMMER

Tiny bursts of morning sun filtered through the foliage and created a kaleidoscopic pattern on the girl's golden hair and the colors of her cotton dress as she strode along the shaded street. Shoulders slumped, head down, her face distorted, she staggered along in the direction of the home of her best friend, Ruth. As she approached, Ruth observed the girl's puffy, tortured features from her living room window and bolted through the doorway. She sprinted up the sidewalk to reach her friend's side before the screen door banged shut behind her.

"Oh, Ruth, we're not going to Okracoke this year."

"Why not, Naomi?"

The sobbing girl did not answer immediately. Ruth held her friend in her arms and waited.

"It's Daniel. He got into trouble at Goldmont. It's part of his punishment."

"But your family always goes to Okracoke the last week in July. What did he do that was so bad?"

"They caught him and some other boys playing cards. Not gambling, just playing cards. And that was his second offense. They said last week he gave a boy some

61

water. The boy was in the stocks. That stupid little bonehead. Everyone knows you don't help people in the stocks. We tried to call him, but they had him in a box, they said, and, anyway, no one is allowed calls at those Bible camps. They whipped him then they put him in some kind of box. He's been in there for three days. I don't know what they're feeding him. Maybe nothing."

Ruth noticed a dark brown van turn the corner and glide silently past the spot where the two young companions stood. Naomi accepted a tissue from her friend and paused to blow her nose before resuming her stroll, in step with Ruth. The sidewalk tilted slightly from the roots of the ancient oaks that stretched their branches to merge with those of their counterparts on the other side. They formed a canopy over the crumbling streets that extended several blocks in both directions. At the corner, they turned south and continued their aimless journey, a familiar route past modest homes nestled in the quiet of the summer morning.

"Your parents must be all to pieces."

"Daddy left work and came home. He and Mama are praying over it."

"How old is Daniel?"

"Thirteen."

"Poor fellow. When did you find out?"

"This morning. A notice from the camp office came in the mail. Mama's going to write and tell Aunt Clara to notify all my aunts and uncles and cousins not to come down this year. I had really been looking forward to seeing all of them again. Now we'll have to wait until next summer."

"I thought they wouldn't allow mail to go to Canada."

"Daddy said we could take it to the post office and have it censored, then pay a special fee of about three hundred dollars and it would get there."

At the intersection they turned right and lifted their dresses above their ankles to circle a mound of concrete and asphalt deposited and forgotten by a street maintenance crew.

"Does Joshua know?"

"I don't know. Sometimes I think he doesn't care about Daniel or the rest of us. All he cares about is the Scouts. I don't even like to be around him anymore."

"Its those camps. I'm told they are unreasonably strict. I'm glad girls aren't allowed to attend."

At Fairmont Street, they turned right once more. As they did so, the two halted abruptly and gasped as they caught sight of the variegated colors in the flower garden inside the fence of the corner lot. The sun's rays bounced about the vast garden and produced shades of gold, red, blue, orange, and purple, a surreal vision that surely brought joy to every soul who passed that way. The gardener, whose silver head appeared among the flowers, did not turn as the two young ladies stopped to admire what was easily the largest and most colorful flower garden in town.

"I love to pass this way just to see this lady's yard."

"Me too. But isn't she a 'switch' or something?"

"I've always heard that, but she must be harmless, or she wouldn't still be here. Somebody who is jealous of her garden probably made up some story or other and spread it around town."

"You're probably right, Naomi. Besides, I've heard that she's almost deaf and that she's not quite right."

They lapsed into silence as their thoughts returned to the misfortune of the Fletcher family. As they strode along on this warm June morning, the two, when viewed from the rear, may have been taken for sisters, perhaps twins, except for their hair color. Both were clad in ankle-length light-colored print dresses and their hair, parted in the middle, swung and bounced, striking the small of their backs as they strode along. The dark brown print of Ruth's dress matched the color of both her hair and her eyes. She was a slim young woman with long, strong limbs, slightly high cheek bones, and a somewhat long nose with nostrils that flared when she smiled or when she

63

became excited. Ruth had moved to Dawson to live with her grandfather and invalid step-grandmother two years before. Her quiet and thoughtful manner, sometimes mistaken for aloofness, prevented her from making friends easily. Naomi had taken her under her wing soon after Ruth arrived, and the two quickly became inseparable.

Naomi's full figure and tan, round face suited her blue eyes and sandy hair. She was a happy young lady, one of the most popular girls at Dawson High. Naomi's mother, Martha, had moved to Dawson eighteen years before when she married Ed, manager of the only bank in town. Housewife and mother of three, Martha volunteered in almost every school and civic activity in town. Now she stood out as a pillar of the community of women of Dawson.

Martha Fletcher's three sisters lived in Canada. Their families had spent the third week in July with Martha's family on Okracoke Island or Bald Head Island since before Naomi was born.

Okracoke and Bald Head were two of a dozen maximum security locations where the United States, for a substantial fee, allowed its citizens to visit Canadian relatives for a maximum of one week per year. Otherwise, no traffic was allowed to cross the border in either direction. The border was closely guarded by the United States military.

The sight of the old lady in the flower garden had reminded Naomi of her friend, also an older lady, who lived over on the east side of town.

"I think I'll go visit Mrs. Price. Would you like to go with me?"

"I don't think so. I'll walk as far as the market with you, but I need to get back and cook lunch for Grandpa."

They continued their journey in silence. There was something about Mrs. Price that made Ruth nervous. Mrs. Price openly questioned authority in a voice too loud for comfort. Sometimes she drank wine, and, worse of all, she had books hidden in her house. Mrs. Price knew that if she

64

ever got caught, she would be arrested. It was almost as if she was daring the Witch Hunters or the Soul Patrol to catch her.

Naomi loved reading Mrs. Price's books. They were the only ones that the teenager had ever seen except the Bible and some hymnals. She admired the rebellious Mrs. Price. Being around her made Naomi feel strong. Though they had never discussed Mrs. Price, Naomi sensed her friend's reluctance and did not insist that Ruth go with her.

The shortest distance from their neighborhood to the home of Mrs. Price was through the ghetto, a sparsely populated area of broken pavement and vacant lots, grown up with china berry and gum trees, wax myrtle, and shoulder-high Johnson grass. A few people made their homes in the ghetto. They lived in tiny nondescript frame houses or in the long, shiny aluminum structures formerly known as mobile homes. The area was paradise for all species that spent their days hunting the rabbits, birds, and insects that lived there.

The girls started as the bushes erupted and a pair of quail emerged and darted skyward, the sound of their whirring wings emitting a sound almost like a scream. Ruth and Naomi chuckled and paused to watch the birds as they disappeared behind the trees in the distance. Neither girl made a comment as they proceeded, but Naomi glanced at her friend and wondered if she were trying to imagine how it would feel to be as free as those birds.

They passed a cluster of three small houses with neatly trimmed lawns and sheets and underwear waving from the clotheslines. Rows of tomato and potato plants and beans and onions lined the neat little gardens in back. Naomi tried to imagine what life was like in Dawson when her grandparents were growing up there. This area, now referred to as the ghetto, was the neighborhood where the poor black residents of Dawson lived before the Great Migration. During the Great Migration, all residents with dark skin fled to Canada or to other foreign countries.

Naomi had never seen a black person except on the video tapes shown at school. The videos always portrayed them as evil, as thieves and murderers who preyed on honest Americans. Naomi suspected that these videos, like many others she had seen at school and at Bible study, stretched the truth to fit the story in order to make a point. After all, her Canadian cousins, the most honest and kind-hearted people she knew, had told her that they had many black friends who were no different than they were. Moreover, they had friends who were Asians, Jews, Muslims, and Indians. In the United States, Canada had become known as "the land of mongrels", but her cousins seemed to actually enjoy living among all these different people.

When they reached the edge of the ghetto, the young women crossed the canal and continued in an easterly direction. Suddenly, two robed figures appeared rounding the corner and moving swiftly in their direction. One man's lean frame and full head of silver hair contrasted sharply to the short, heavy figure and large bald head of his companion. The two men were headed for the powder-blue Cadillac parked up ahead. It was the first new car the girls had seen in some time. The chrome trim and bumper reflected the midday sun.

As the girls neared the car, they recognized Reverend Mills and Reverend Wade in their new robes, attire recently adopted by the North Carolina clergy. The purpose of the robes was to give them the appearance of medieval monks, but they seemed out of place on such a warm summer day. Reverend Wade spoke in a stern voice.

"Good afternoon, sister Fletcher and sister ...."

"Hoffstetler, I believe," said Reverend Mills.

"Hoffstetter," corrected Naomi. "Good afternoon, Reverend Mills, Reverend Wade. I hope you are both in good health. I like your new robes. They look very distinguished."

"What are the two of you doing over in this

neighborhood?"

"We are just out for a walk, sir. Is anything wrong?"

"Girls your age need to be at home helping your mothers....say, Miss Hoffstetter, what is your first name?"

"Ruth, sir."

"Ruth, you live with your grandparents over on Wilson Street? Carlton Graham, isn't it?"

"Yes sir."

"Is Mr. Graham still working at the hardware store?"

"Yes sir."

"Where do you go to church?"

"Saint James Episcopal, downtown."

"Episcopal. I should have guessed. Your congregation is shrinking, isn't it?"

"Reverend Mills, we have an appointment," Reverend Wade interrupted.

"Very well. Girls, get on back home, now. Naomi, I want to see more of you at evening worship services."

"Yes sir."

"Go with God, girls."

"Go with God, Reverend Mills, Reverend Wade," said the two girls, in unison.

They watched the Cadillac as it disappeared in the distance then turned to resume their journey.

"Go on home, my ass."

"Naomi! I've never heard such language from you!"

"Doggone it, Ruth, they make me so mad. It was men like them that whipped my brother. Don't they make you angry?"

"Yes, but I don't think it's too good an idea to speak that way about the clergy."

Naomi wondered what Mrs. Price would say about the incident.

* * *

"Why, the nerve of those pompous jackasses," exclaimed Helen Price. "It's that same arrogant, 'Christian' attitude in those camp directors that is responsible for the wretched way your poor little brother is being treated. I feel real sorry for him, but if he is anything like his sister, he'll be just fine."

She released her young friend from her grand-motherly embrace. Naomi had burst into tears once more as she unloaded her burden to the one adult that she felt would understand. Gray, but not too gray, Ellen Price was a lively sixty-year-old of medium height with ample breasts and hips and a little too thick around the waist, but still what many would consider shapely. She had a twinkle in her knowing hazel eyes, a quick, broad smile, and a knack for making people laugh and for making them feel comfortable.

Helen wore a print dress one size too small that exposed her shapely calves when she sat. Naomi had seen worse. Once Naomi had found her in shorts that stopped short of her knees and a naughty shirt that exposed her arms and back. She would have been ar-rested if she had been caught like that, of course, even in her home, but this act was consistent with her habit of ignoring the rules.

She held a glass of wine in her hand when Naomi arrived, also a criminal offense.

"What you need, young lady, is a tall glass of this very excellent white wine." She refilled her glass.

"No, thank you. I need to get back home to comfort Mom and Dad."

"How about some ice tea?"

"No, really. Thank you."

"You mentioned that the two preachers were interested in Ruth. Why didn't she come with you? She doesn't like being in my home, does she?"

"Yes, she does. She had to go to the grocery store for her grandfather. By the way, we passed that flower garden on Fairmont Street. It's more beautiful than ever this summer."

"You mean Mrs. Thompson. Her flower garden is legendary. Do you know her very well?"

"I don't know her at all. I don't know anybody that knows much about her. I heard that she might be a 'switch'. Have you ever heard that?"

"A 'suspected witch'? What on God's green earth is a 'suspected witch'? And why would anyone in his right mind accuse a deaf, harmless old lady like Mrs. Thompson of being a witch?

"I want you to stop by there and introduce yourself sometime, honey. You'll see."

* * *

"Hey, Naomi, wait up!" It was Joshua, on his bicycle. So why did someone on foot need to wait up for someone riding a bicycle? What a dumbass, Naomi thought.

"What's wrong?" her brother asked.

"I'm worried about Daniel. What else?"

"Why is everybody so tore up about Daniel? It was just ordinary punishment for a wise guy that can't obey the rules. I've seen some boys get a lot worse. It's about time somebody put the fear of God into that little rebel."

"Just hush. I don't want to hear your dumbass crap today."

"Watch that nasty mouth, girl. One word from me, and you know what will happen."

"Has Mama quit crying yet?"

"No, and she hasn't cooked supper or nothing. Her and Daddy just sit there and don't say anything."

Joshua had dismounted and was walking his bike alongside his older sister. Joshua talked big, but Naomi knew he was concerned about their younger brother, too. At fifteen, Joshua was taller than his father and still growing. His sun-bleached blond hair was cut short, and when he smiled, he looked like his sister. The two had been very close growing up, but Joshua had changed in the last two years, it seemed to Naomi. She thought it was the influence of the summer camps. He had attended them for three weeks for each of the past two summers and had just returned home the previous week.

"Did you hear about the witch they burned up in Raleigh last Saturday?"

The council had tried to change the name of the state's capital, but they couldn't agree on a new name, so it was still Raleigh.

"Ben said they tied her to a big wheel about the size of a ferris wheel and rolled it into a gigantic fire. His uncle saw it. He said there was a big crowd and everybody cheered."

"How horrible!"

"I knew you would say that. It's the only way to wipe them out. Otherwise the demons will come back and take over the soul of somebody else. Ben says they have witch-burnings once a month up in D.C. He said sometimes they burn four or five the same night."

"That is so unbelievable... those poor women. They ought to burn those nasty Witch Hunters."

"Careful, Sis! Keep your voice down!"

"Please don't mention this to Mama. Not now."

Martha, their mother, didn't handle bad news very well. When Joshua had come home last year and told her about the bomb that exploded on the train in Toronto and killed more than a dozen people, she had become so upset that she went to bed and stayed for two days.

"It was the Sword of David, for sure," Joshua had said, "That will teach those decadent mongrels a lesson."

The Sword was a secret society made up of mostly ex-Scouts who didn't qualify to be Witch Hunters. There was a rumor that some were army commandos.

In the Fletcher home, one could almost taste the gloom that hung in the air like fog in the woods on a September morning. The house was a two-story Victorian from the first decade of the previous century. The large front door opened into a wide hall with a high ceiling and spacious living rooms on either side. On the floor of the room on the left, usually referred to as the parlor, Martha sat and leaned back on a sofa that had seen better days. Her husband leaned forward from the large chair facing her. The only sound was the ticking of the ancient clock on the mantle.

"Hello, you two."

"Hi, Ma. Hi, Daddy."

"You'll have to make yourself a sandwich for supper. There's tuna fish and baloney and a little of that ham left. There are a few beets left, and you can warm up those string beans."

"I'm not hungry," replied Naomi. Joshua had already found his way to the kitchen.

"You need to eat something, honey."

"Oh, Mama, I'm so tired of the spies, and the meanness, and the tension, all in the name of Christianity. Why can't we go to Canada like your family?"

Her father's jaw fell and her mother's wide eyes and red face communicated her alarm as she pointed to the light fixture on the ceiling. Everyone knew about the listening devises in every home in the country, but Naomi just didn't care. Let them come and get her.

"Naomi Fletcher, I know you're tired and worried about your brother, but that is no excuse for that kind of talk," Martha finally said. "Go to bed immediately, and I expect an apology to your father and to me in the morning."

* * *

Daniel returned in the middle of July, just when they were supposed to have gone to the beach. He seemed none the worse for his ordeal, but the fact that he was responsible for the cancellation of his family's vacation weighed heavily on the thirteen-year-old's mind. Martha's sunny disposition had returned, and the family was, for the most part, back to normal.

The extra time that Naomi found on her hands was spent reading *Huckleberry Finn, Little Women,* and *Silas*

71

Marner over at Mrs. Price's house. And on those leisurely journeys through town with her best friend, Ruth. Each outing seemed to find them on Fairmont Street at the flower garden. Naomi had told her friend about what Mrs. Price had had to say about the gardener, Mrs. Thompson, and the girls decided to pay the old lady a visit to tell her how much they admired her work. They did so on a typically sultry August afternoon. They rang and waited patiently on the porch, rang again and then a third time before turning to depart. Just then the hinges of the door squealed faintly as it opened a few inches. A stooped, gray figure appeared, barely visible in the semi-darkness. The old woman squinted at the visitors a few seconds then swung the door open a little wider and spoke in a thin, brittle voice.

"For a minute I thought you were my nieces from Greensboro come to visit. They haven't been in a good while. Anyhow, I see now you're not them. How can I help you girls?"

"Mrs. Thompson, I'm Naomi Fletcher and this is Ruth Hofstetter. We were sent by Mrs. Price. We wanted to tell you how much we enjoy seeing your flowers."

"What's that? You were sent by Christ?"

"Mrs. Price," Naomi almost shouted.

"Price, Price. I'm so sorry. Where did you come from?"

"Mrs. Thompson, we live right here in Dawson. We have just never had a chance to meet you and we stopped to do so." The volume of the quiet-spoken Ruth's voice surprised Naomi.

"Good. I'm glad you came by. What is Mrs. Price's first name?"

"Let's see. Helen, I think. Isn't that it, Ruth?"

"Yes, I think you told me it was Helen. Do you know her, Mrs. Thompson?"

"Helen Price......The name doesn't ring a bell. Lives here in town, huh? Who did she marry?"

"I'm not sure, Mrs. Thompson. She has never

72

talked about her husband to me. Ruth here has only met her twice."

"I used to know some Prices over around Kinston years ago. You say she sent you to meet me?"

"Well, she suggested that we stop."

"No matter. You are welcome to see my garden. Go on around back, and I'll go through the house and see if I can find some ice tea."

As the girls returned to the sidewalk which led to the gate on the left side of the house, Naomi noticed a break in the hedge next to the house and the two slipped through to the back yard. As they wound their way past the head-high hedge that separated the front yard from the garden, their path took them close to the chimney, and Naomi noticed two black cables running up though the ivy. She glanced up, expecting to see a television antenna, but there was none. Then Mrs. Thompson came out with a pitcher of tea, and the cables were forgotten.

The garden was astonishing, even in the heat of August. Their hostess named each plant as she showed them around. Many of the names were new to the girls. It was a beautiful afternoon, almost cool in the shade of the two towering oaks. Naomi wondered how such a frail old lady could manage all the work necessary to maintain such a huge garden. She asked, but Mrs. Thompson didn't hear the question. In fact, Mrs. Thompson didn't do much talking after the tour was over. Only once, when she and Ruth were alone in the far corner of the garden did the old lady seem to come to life.

"What were you two talking so much about?" asked Naomi as they headed home.

"Nothing much. When she found out that I was fairly new in town, she wanted to know who my family was and where we came from."

"She's an odd old lady."

"I like her."

"I like her, too, but she's so old and feeble. Just kind of out-to-lunch."

Daniel was restless. "I'm going for a bike ride. You want to go, Nami?"

His wink meant he wanted to talk out of earshot of the ever-present listening devices inside the house. When they got to the ghetto, they dismounted and walked along a dirt path toward the big orange setting sun.

"Why are we here, Sis? Why aren't we in Canada with our cousins?"

"Why, I guess it's because this is our home."

"I hate it here. I'm not the only one, either. Some of the boys I met at camp are talking about escaping to Canada. Have you ever heard of Harriet Tubman?"

"No."

"She was a black slave here in the United States in the eighteen hundreds. She escaped to the north, where slavery was illegal and she was free. Then she went back and helped her family escape."

"They had slaves in the United States?"

"Yeah. Here in North Carolina and some other southern states. All the black people were slaves, brought over here from Africa to work in the fields.

"The boys at camp told you this?"

"Just the four guys that hate it here like I do. Anyway, Harriet set up a system to lead a few slaves at the time to freedom. They called it the Underground Railroad."

"Is there an underground railroad to help people escape to Canada?"

"That's what some people are saying."

"How do you think they could get away with it? If they get caught, they would be executed for sure."

"We could be executed for doing nothing."

"What do you mean?"

"They can make you disappear without a trial or even an arrest. You just are never heard from again."

"That can't be. Are you sure?"

"I met a boy named Benjamin from Godsboro. He

says it used to be named Goldsboro. Anyhow, he named about seven or eight people that had disappeared over the past five years."

Naomi wondered about the father of her friend, Rebekah Phillips. Also, Mr. and Mrs. Edmondson. The rumor was that they suddenly decided to move to Philadelphia, and they left their house, clothing, and all furniture and personal items behind. The incident seemed very strange. No plausible explanation was offered.

Her brother continued, "In Canada, they can't arrest you unless they charge you with something, and you are considered innocent until they prove you did it."

Naomi knew this to be true. Her cousins were always bragging about Canada when they stayed together at the beach. They also described TV programs that showed news from Europe and Asia, people with no clothes, using blasphemous language. They had small computers of their own, books, and electric service and telephone service that was almost never interrupted. There people felt free to behave outrageously, even to publicly criticize their government leaders. Women were not only allowed to work, but were hired to perform the jobs of men. And their swimsuits! They exposed almost everything!

What a scandalous, irreverent bunch the Canadian cousins were. But so free, and so much fun! She thought back to a dark summer evening on Okracoke the year she turned fourteen. They were out on the porch, just a few yards from the waves rolling in at high tide.

"You sure are growing yourself a nice pair of tits, Nami. You should try on one of Paula's swimsuits so we can admire all that beauty you keep hidden under those long dresses."

It was her cousin Vincent, sixteen years old and not known for his good manners.

"Vincent Edwards, if you don't shut that filthy bazoo of yours, I'm going to shut it for you." It was Paula Brown, another cousin, Naomi's confidant and her idol. Paula was a year older than Vincent. There were eight cousins in all with four different last names because they were the offspring of four sisters. Martha was number three.

"I'm almost sorry I'm your cuz, Cuz. If I wasn't I'd surely invite you to the Saturday night dance, if they had one in this outrageously swinging country of yours."

"Vincent, dammit, leave Nami alone."

"What a bunch of pricks you've got running this deadass country. The highlight of the trip so far has been the U.S. Airlines stewardess was actually wearing a little makeup."

"If she was talking to you, she was probably blushing from embarrassment."

"Please, Vincent, you are not in Canada." Naomi pointed to the ceiling where the listening devices were usually concealed.

"Now, you know if they are listening, there's not a damn thing they can do because they'd have to admit that they were listening, which is a violation of the international agreement. So, up your nose with a rubber hose, Mr. Witch Hunter Nazi and the same to all your pig dung eating friends!"

"Vincent, please!"

"I hope they are listening and that they bring their dumb butts around here. God will not prevent my big fat foot from stomping their sanctimonious asses. And if I can't handle the job, Daniel and George can."

Daniel and George, the two ten-year-olds, had been laughing so hard that they were literally in tears.

How Naomi missed seeing her cousins this year. She also missed hearing first-hand about the evil nation to the north. Beer and wine, bawdy TV shows from Europe, dancing, gambling, lewd jokes, books, and people dressed in shorts and tee-shirts. All evil tools of the devil, forbidden in the United States, they were not only legal in Canada, they were commonplace. Evil, corrupt, a land of anti-Christian mongrels and devil worshippers. Well, I'm sorry, God, she thought, but I just have a hard time believing that my cousins are bad. Forgive me for thinking this dear Lord, but if the Canadians are devil worshippers, his disciples have a lot more fun than yours do.

"Ben said a boy who lives in his neighborhood turned in his own parents to the Soul Patrol. They were put in stocks in the town square and the woman almost died," Daniel was saying.

There they were, leaving the ghetto, crossing the canal, just as Naomi and Ruth had done several weeks before. And there was the sky blue Cadillac, parked in the same spot on the same block.

"Will you look at that car! It's got to be owned by some government official. I'll bet I could drive it. I wish we could afford something more than those two old pieces of junk we have."

Naomi did not tell him that she knew who owned the Cadillac. It would just make him more angry. She was beginning to fear for her little brother's safety.

They mounted their bikes and turned left to begin their return home the long way around. This was the street on which Mrs. Price lived, of course, and Naomi looked for her friend as they approached her two-story home. Naomi did not really expect to see her, but, suddenly, there she was, coming from the huge brick home on the corner, turning quickly away from the on-coming bicyclists, striding briskly down the sidewalk toward her own more modest dwelling.

"Hi, Mrs. Price!" Naomi called as she approached the bouncing figure. Her shout was the result of a sudden impulse of mischievousness, and the start from the victim was no surprise to Naomi. But she was not prepared for the intensity of the reaction, the high-pitched little scream, and the hands to the chest as Mrs. Price doubled over. When she looked up, she recognized the blond rider circling back with a look of concern on her face.

"My lord, girl, you gave me a scare!"

"I'm so sorry, Mrs. Price. My brother and I were just out for a ride and I happened to see you come out of the big house on the corner."

77

She came to a stop next to the curb where the older woman stood. Daniel circled and stopped beside her.

"Well, I don't know what made me jump so. I just didn't hear you two coming up on me. I was just over checking up on my neighbor. She's a widow who lives there all alone and she's been sick.

"Well, now. You must be Daniel. I'm Mrs. Price."

"Hello. I'm pleased to meet you."

"You children come on in the house. I'll see what I can find for a snack."

"No, thank you, ma'am. We've got to head on back home so I can help my mother with supper. I'm so sorry I startled you," said Naomi.

"Don't give it another thought. You two come back when you can stay. Bye, now."

"Bye, Mrs. Price."

With that she quickly resumed her march to her house a few feet away.

When the two reached the next intersection, they paused to allow three automobiles and a truck to pass, on their way out of town. As they waited, Daniel suggested that they ride by the high school. The churches used the facilities at the school for their summer softball games, and the spectators usually included numerous teenagers, some from surrounding communities. They turned right and rode out the mile or so to the school, only to find that they were an hour too early for the night's game. The team from rural Tolson's Neck Free Will Baptist was to play the locals at New Hope Christian. The bicyclists circled the vacant field and headed for home via a narrow street that paralleled the main artery. This route brought them back past the back yard of the big brick house from which Mrs. Price had emerged half an hour before. Two robed figures appeared at the back door and moved rapidly around the corner toward the powder blue Cadillac in the distance. Naomi slowed and hissed at her brother.

"What?"

"Shh! Come here."

"What is it?"

"Those two preachers in the robes were Reverend Mills and Reverend Wade. That blue Cadillac over on the other street belongs to Reverend Wade."

"Go on! That was the same house that your old lady friend came out of. I thought she didn't like those old holy rollers."

"I don't know. Maybe she was leaving because they arrived."

But why didn't she mention it? And why were they coming out the back door? Why did they park two blocks away? Naomi tried to dismiss the incident over the next few days, but there was something about it that she just couldn't get out of her mind. She rode past the house frequently in the days that followed, and her observations perplexed her even more. There were comings and goings of men, day and night, dressed in robes, business suites, and work clothes. Some nights she found the house dark, but on others there were lights on all three floors. Then, most puzzling of all, she saw a dark van almost hidden among the fruit trees and shrubbery of the back yard of the brick house. It was the type that most people associated with the Soul Patrol. Naomi didn't know what was going on in the big house, but she was certain that the sick widow lady didn't live there alone. She decided not to share her observations with Ruth or Daniel, but she sure wished that she could tell someone.

* * *

"Vince, my man, what a day, huh? Christ, this place is beautiful! If it wasn't in such a fouled-up, God-forsaken country, I'd think about moving down here."

It was Raymond Lebeau, husband of Martha's baby sister, Hannah. He and Vincent were on the deck just below Naomi's seat on the deck off the third floor bedroom that she shared with Paula. They did not realize that Naomi was in the dark above them. The sea breeze picked up their voices and made it impossible for her not to eavesdrop.

"Do you believe what they have done to this country? Christ, Vinnie, they used to have everything we have and more. Did you ever hear my dad talk about the Great Migration?"

"We saw a lot of old tapes in my history class."

"Dad was in Toronto when they started arriving. My bother Charlie remembers it. The European Union had planes over here flying the Jews, black people, and Asians out of here, not to mention over half the white folks. He said you couldn't get a flight out of Paris or London. They almost went to war when that 747 was shot down over Atlanta. If they had shot down one or two more, this might be a European colony now. Again. The people here would be a hell of a lot better off."

"I couldn't believe the book burnings. They said the pile of books in New York was so high you could see it from miles away and it burned for six months."

"Incredible. Hand me another beer, will you Vinnie? ... And now, they spend all their resources keeping people in, keeping people out, spying on their own citizens, jamming the airways, and fighting that damned civil war in Hawaii. Meanwhile, the whole country is crumbling and falling down around their ears."

"They say they still accuse people of being witches and burn them alive."

"And people still disappear overnight. There is no telling how many."

"Incredible."

* * *

Naomi tried the bell again. Still no answer. She peered into the dark hallway of Hofstetter home. Silence. The blinds were down all around, and the grass was above her ankles. She had not seen Ruth in over a week. Naomi's friend was not enrolled in school, and the administration received no request for her records to be sent to another school. No one had answered the phone or the doorbell during that time. When Naomi saw the reflection of the dark van cruising by, she turned and stalked off in the opposite direction. She was crying. "Dorks!" She spoke aloud.

* * *

Two days later there had been no word from Ruth or her family. Her absence had not alarmed anyone at school. Her teachers and her classmates believed that Ruth and her grandparents had simply moved away during the summer. The paper work would be along any day. Naomi knew better, however, as did Joshua and Daniel. All feared the worst, even Joshua. Ruth, her grandfather, and his invalid wife would never be heard from again. To think that it could happen here in little Dawson, to someone they knew, to a friend, was a sobering thought. What was the girl's offense? Naomi was beginning to face the fact that she didn't really know much about Ruth. Did Naomi's association with the missing girl make Naomi a target? And her family? Had she placed her family in peril?

Naomi decided in desperation to ask Mrs. Thompson, the flower lady, if she knew anything about Ruth's whereabouts. Naomi had not seen the old woman since that first visit to her house and garden, but Ruth had been back several times and the two had become friends.

The next day Naomi stepped up on the porch of the old house on Fairfield Street. She rang the bell and waited. Finally, the door was nudged open. Mrs. Thompson's withered figure barely visible in the dark interior through the narrow opening.

"Oh, it's Mrs. Price's friend. How is she doing?"

Mrs. Price? Why was she Mrs. Price's friend?

"Oh. I'm sorry, I haven't seen Mrs. Price in about a month. I'm here about Ruth Hofstetter. She didn't come to school this week, and no one answers her door. Have you seen her?"

"No, honey. I haven't seen her in some time."

The door swung to a half-open position. There was a long silence. The old woman's stare was intense, but sympathetic. As the old lady studied her, Naomi burst into tears. The door opened, and Mrs. Thompson stepped out onto the porch and took the girl into her arms.

"Meet me in the back," she whispered.

She brought out tea once again and they sat and made small talk. Naomi wept once more when the conversation returned to the whereabouts of Ruth. Naomi found the old woman to be a good listener, much more alert than Naomi remembered her to be during that first visit. They strolled around the garden, and the conversation turned to Mrs. Price. The old woman took the girl's arm and dropped her voice as she continued to probe. Naomi had no idea why she did so, but she found herself telling her about seeing Mrs. Price coming from the big brick house that day while riding with Daniel. She also told about the preachers they saw leaving from the same house and about the vans and all the other activity. Mrs. Thompson listened and nodded. Naomi wondered why she had thought that this lady was old and slow. She not only understood the things that Naomi was telling her, but none of it seemed to surprise her. Who was this person? Naomi was glad she had come.

They had stopped in the far corner of the garden. "Thank you for coming to visit me, Naomi," the old woman said finally. "You are a fine young lady. It's time you went home. Please do this again, soon."

"Thank you for listening. I see why Ruth came here so often."

The old woman suddenly stopped, put her fingers to her lips, and stooped to pick up a potted plant and shift it to one side. After the second and third plants had been moved, she drew a small chalk board from the sand where the plants had stood. She found a piece of chalk in her apron pocket and began to write. When Naomi read the message, her gasp and giggle brought a stern look from the old woman, a thin finger at her lips once more.

The message read, "Ruth is safe in Canada."

BUS TO D.C.

Barbara Sawyer, ace reporter for the Barclay Post, squeezed her steering wheel and resisted the urge to blow her horn at the minivan up ahead or to bulldoze her way up on the sidewalk and around the stalled traffic into the Murphy High School parking lot. She had left the newspaper office in plenty of time to make the morning assembly, but she had not anticipated the size of the crowd. She scratched her head and reached to turn the air conditioner up a notch. It was not nine o'clock, but the moisture that formed on her scalp threatened to creep down her neck. The cars clogged both lanes of the circular drive like a giant serpent that wound its way slowly in the direction of the sweltering campus parking lot. The crowd had come to offer support to the family of Phillip J. Zarsa, Jr., star quarterback, honors student, popular class president, and now a missing person.

When Barbara finally reached the stop sign, she wheeled to the left and sped down the narrow back road to the school bus parking lot at the rear of the main building.

She braked to avoid plowing her white Contour into a cluster of laughing adolescents who dashed around the buses. She parked the car and followed them past the row of mobile classrooms to the side door of the gymnasium.

Barbara knew her way around the Murphy campus. She had visited the school many times in her high school days as a member of archival Masonboro High's volleyball team and as a spectator at other sporting events. Entering the gym brought back memories of her glory days as an athlete during a time that was otherwise four years of misery. Her team had usually gotten their butts kicked whenever they came here. She wondered if that had changed.

Barbara entered the gym at the rear, behind the temporary stage at one end of the basketball court. The student body filled the bleachers on both sides and spilled out on the floor five or six deep the length of the court. A student stood at the podium and sang *The Star-Spangled Banner*.

Behind the singer principal Frank Dawson stood at attention with his hand over his heart. He was a short black man with a thin mustache and a newly trimmed flattop hair cut. Several other adults who Barbara recognized as city council members stood behind the principal along with three members of the local school board. The crowd's attention focused on the Junior ROTC color guard assembled in the center of the gym and the flag of the United States held high by a young lady almost as tall as Barbara. A woman with short red hair in a black dress and heels spoke into a walkie-talkie and moved to where Barbara had stopped. She peered at the press pass that Barbara presented and offered a grim smile and nod before returning to her position at the corner of the bleachers. Frank Dawson recognized the elected officials and parents and thanked them for coming. He spoke calmly into the microphone, and all present listened quietly.

"Last Friday morning, April 17, something very

85

strange happened. One of our students, Phil Zarsa, known to many of you as 'Zorro', disappeared. He was with the seniors on board a bus en route to New York City for our annual senior trip. We don't know what happened. He was on board one minute, and the next he was not. It happened in northern Virginia, south of Washington, DC. The Spotsylvania County sheriff's department continues to conduct an investigation in cooperation with our own Barclay Police Department.

"We have with us today Detective Sergeant Frank Delucca who is heading the investigation. He and his officers will be with us all morning to answer any questions that you have and perhaps to ask you some. We are asking for your full cooperation as they conduct their investigation.

"The seniors who were on their way to New York are back with us today, at least some of them. The trip was cancelled and they returned home last Thursday. We'd like to welcome them back today. We're glad you're safely back home. We understand that this is an emotional experience and that some found the assembly too painful to attend. We trust that they will return to us later in the day.

"We will now get an update on the investigation from Sergeant Delucca. Sergeant?"

Delucca was also short, but he was heavier than the principal. His brown suit fit as if it were tailored, but it looked too heavy for the weather outside.

"Ladies and gentlemen, after four days of intensive investigation, I regret to report that we do not know what happened to Mr. Zarsa, and we do not know his whereabouts at this time. If any students feel that they have information that may be useful in our investigation, please come forward after the assembly. We will be available all morning, and we can come back tomorrow if needed.

"This is a perplexing case, unlike any case I've seen. The Spotsylvania Sheriff Department has combed a fifty-mile radius around the location of the bus when Mr.

Zarsa was reported missing. They have requested that the FBI send a team down to assist them. They are awaiting a reply. Each student who was a passenger on the bus has been questioned several times, as they can tell you. We have not found a kidnap message. There is no evidence that young Zarsa has fled his home under his own power.

"Still, we are cautiously optimistic. There is no reason to suspect the worse. There is no evidence of foul play. Are there any questions?"

The murmur of the crowd subsided when the principal returned to the podium.

"If any of you have questions, now is your opportunity to ask them. Stand and raise your hand, and one of the vice principals will come to you with a microphone."

A clamor erupted as a dozen students stood to speak.

"Wait, I'm not finished..Listen..Listen.." He waited for quiet to return.

"This is not easy for any of us. Please remain calm and show respect for your neighbors and fellow students."

The first student spoke loudly into the microphone as the crowd began to buzz once again.

"Mr. Dawson, there are so many rumors out there. We want to hear from the people on the bus. How did it happen? Where were you stopped?"

"Yeah!" several people shouted.

The din increased when one of the senior trip chaperones, Mr. Panetta, emerged from the crowd and strode to the stage. A retired marine helicopter pilot and now a lead teacher in the math department, Mr. Panetta was a favorite among the students. Quiet returned as he reached the podium on the stage.

"My name is Mr. Panetta," he said. "I was a chaperone and a passenger on the second bus. The chaperones from the first bus, the one from which Phil disappeared, are not present. This has been very difficult for all of us. I hope you'll understand.

"First, we were not stopped when your friend,

Phillip Zarsa, vanished. The last time anyone on board saw him, he was entering the bathroom."

It was several minutes before the noise level subsided and he could continue.

"At some point between ten and fifteen minutes later his friends, concerned, began to knock on the door. There was no reply. The three teachers on board began to call to him and pound on the door. Still there was no reply. Finally, we stopped the buses at a truck stop and forced the door open. The bathroom was empty."

The crowd gasped, in spite of the fact that most of the students had heard at least one version of the story during the previous three days. Barbara headed for the door. She wanted to move quickly. She had some ideas.

She was on her cell phone before she reached the main highway.

"Hilda, can you do me a favor? Call LaGrange Bus Company in La Grange and find out the name of the bus drivers who were driving the Murphy High School seniors to New York. Get the home address of the one that drove the lead bus."

"Will do. Should I call you back on your cell phone?"

"Yes, please. Thanks."

Barbara turned right onto the highway, took the bypass around town, and headed west, the direction of La Grange. She stopped at the Trade station to buy gas and grab a cup of coffee. She pulled back on the highway just as Hilda called.

"The driver's name is Clarence Harris. He lives in Greene County, off Highway 13 between Snow Hill and Goldsboro." She read the address.

"He has the day off, but he may not be there. Channel Nine just left the bus company office to go look for him. CNN interviewed him yesterday.

"And you may want to know that the driver is coming in to work tomorrow. He and another driver are going back up to Virginia to bring the bus back. The sheriff up there is releasing it tomorrow. Channel Seven is following the drivers up there in their van."

"Thanks, Hilda. Does Brian know all this?"

"He's standing right here. Hold on. He wants to speak to you."

Brian James was the editor. He had moved to Barclay from central Florida two years ago to take the job. He worked hard and he demanded the same from his staff members. His energy and enthusiasm were contagious. Barbara liked him.

"Hi, Barb. Were you able to talk to any of the chaperones or students?"

"No, Brian. They aren't back at school. I was hoping to talk to the driver this morning and return to the school later. How do you feel about my going to Virginia and talking to the sheriff up there and looking at the area where it happened?"

"It may be late for that. We're watching CNN now. We'll talk about that later today. I tell you what, Barbara, I know Frank Dawson pretty well. Why don't I give him a call and see what I can set up for you? You go to Greene County and try for the driver, then meet me back here and we'll do some brainstorming and come up with a plan."

"Will do. Thanks for the help. I'll see you in a couple of hours."

89

Thirty minutes later Barbara was knocking on the door of a small brick home in rural Greene County. After ten minutes she gave up and tried next door. The stooped, gray-haired lady who answered the door informed her that Clarence Harris did indeed live next door. She said he usually visited his mother in Goldsboro on his days off.

"Ma'am, I need to ask you a big favor. I'm a newspaper reporter from over in Barclay. I wanted to talk to Mr. Harris about something that happened on his bus last Friday."

"Honey, I figured tha's who you was. They been lookin' him all weekend. Started Saturday mornin' early. He tol' the story about three times, and he got tired of it so he took off. You want me to call his mama's and see if I can get 'im on the phone?"

"Would you? That would be wonderful."

The woman's eyes twinkled as she motioned with her frail dark hand, and Barbara followed her through a spacious, tastefully furnished living room into a small but immaculate kitchen. There she poured them two cups of coffee and picked up the portable phone to dial a number she knew by heart.

"Busy," she said.

Fifteen minutes, two more busy signals, and a second cup of coffee later, Barbara was on the road again. When she reached the intersection at Highway 13, she hesitated. Right to Goldsboro, or left to Snow Hill and back to Barclay? She turned left.

"You can't hit a home run every time, old girl," she said out loud. She was determined not to feel sorry for herself. Five years out of UNC's prestigious school of journalism, with honors, and she was still covering town board meetings and ribbon cuttings for new bank branches and convenience stores. And now something like this comes along and she doesn't even hear about it until two days after it happened. And now she can't find anybody because they're hiding from the press.

She was rounding the curve at the massage parlor

next door to the liquor store just outside Snow Hill. She picked up the phone, but it rang before she could dial.

"Barbara, honey, you need to come to Masonboro as soon as possible." It was her mother. "Everybody's okay, but you need to come home. It's urgent. Your grandmother's here with some friends. We need to talk to you right away."

"Mom, I'll try to get there tonight. I'm involved in a story. Tell Grandmama I'll get by her house soon."

"Barbara, we need you now. This is not about your grandmother. It's about you and these people and your future. Please. Trust me. This is for you."

What the hell was she talking about?

"Sorry, Mama, I just can't come now. This is the story of the year. I'll explain when I see you. I'll be there as soon as I can."

"Honey, please believe me. You need to come home now. Please stop somewhere and call me."

"Okay, Mama. I'll call in to the office, then I'll call you back."

Barbara disconnected and dialed the newspaper. Hilda answered.

"Hilda, is Brian close by?"

"Barbara, he's gone out to the school with Kevin. But, listen. You need to call your mother right away. She sounds frantic. She needs you right away."

"What is it? Did she tell you?"

"No, but you need to call her now."

"Okay, Hilda. I'll swing by Masonboro on my way back. Tell Brian I'll be at the office by noon. Thanks for your help."

She pointed the little car toward Masonboro and called to let her mother know she was on the way.

Thirty minutes later she exited the freeway to take the old Greenville highway into the town where Barbara's family had made their home for several generations. Many of the familiar landmarks had been replaced by new subdivisions, banks, and office buildings. Automobile dealerships, convenience stores, and shopping centers, all single-story structures, had sprung up in recent months. As she stopped at the light in front of Mason Park Mall she recalled summers working in the tobacco fields that had now been replaced by parking lots for shoppers. She and her teenage friends had sat on the porch of the old country store and enjoyed Vienna sausages and cheese and crackers for lunch. That site was now occupied by either Applebee's or Burger King. She wasn't quite sure.

After a three-minute wait in the left turn lane, she turned on Masonboro Boulevard and drove one-half mile to turn right at the Masonboro County Club sign. The ancient oak and maple trees lined both sides of the streets and shielded the two-story homes that stood so far back from the street that passersby could catch only glimpses of them among the foliage. These homes were constructed at a time when Masonboro was a small town whose primary purpose was to provide a market place for the tobacco farmers in the county. Barbara's father had owned one of the mammoth tobacco warehouses where buyers from Reynolds and Liggett-Myers and American and all the others came to bid on the golden piles of carefully wrapped leaf laid out in the endless rows under the dirty skylights.

Barbara wondered what she was doing here on a day when the biggest story of her life was breaking over in Barclay. Was she subconsciously running from the hot seat? Turning it over to Brian and Kevin? She didn't think so, but here she was. There was just something in her mother's tone. Some sense that she must come. She had trained her mother to never, never, never say anything important when Barbara was on the cell phone. But why in hell couldn't Barbara just stop and call from a phone booth?

"W.E. Sawyer" the mailbox read, as it had since Barbara was a little girl, even though Mr. William Edward Sawyer had been dead for four years. The driveway was a semicircle of little stones that made a crunching sound when crunched by a set of automobile tires. Myrtle Sawyer met her daughter out at the car before she could park and get the door open.

"Barbara, this is your big break," she said, pulling her from the car. "Inside that house is none other than the grandmother, great aunt, and mother of the young man who disappeared last Friday. The mother wants to talk to you about it. To tell you her story."

Barbara's knees went weak. Her heart fluttered and began to pound in her ears. She could only smile down at her mother who was five inches shorter than she was. They grasped each other and embraced then turned and hurried toward the house. Barbara stopped and rushed back to retrieve her notebook and tape recorder from the front seat. She found her reflection in the window of her car and brushed her hair with her fingers.

Barbara's grandmother met them at the front door and made the introductions when they were inside. Her best friend was there with her niece, Yvonne Zarsa, mother of Phillip Zarsa, the lost boy. It had been this long -time friend of Barbara's grandmother who suggested that Yvonne talk to Barbara.

Yvonne, a slender woman with dark hair that tumbled to her shoulders, sat at the dining room table behind a large glass of ice tea. She did not rise when Barbara and her mother entered. When they were introduced, Barbara took the woman's thin fingers and peered into her sad gray eyes set deeply in dark sockets. Barbara settled in the chair next to her. The hint of a smile appeared on Yvonne's thin, colorless lips when she spoke.

"I wanted to tell someone my story. Someone who would listen and write it for everyone to read. I just don't want to face dozens of reporters, all shouting insulting questions. Questions that I don't know the answer to."

"Ms. Zarsa, I'm very sorry about your loss, though it may not be a permanent loss. I can't imagine how you must feel."

They were all seated at the table now. Myrtle had poured tea all around.

"Ms. Zarsa, what is it that you want to tell me?"

"Phillip is our only son. He is one of the finest people I ever met in my life. My husband and I devoted our lives to taking care of Phil, to make sure that he turned out right. We were so proud of that young man. He had decided to attend the Naval Academy, you know. He wanted to be an officer in the Marines, like his father."

"When did you find out about his disappearance?" Barbara asked.

"Mr. Panetta, the chaperone that broke into the bathroom, called my husband at work. My husband called me at the courthouse. I work for the Clerk of Court. My husband is not taking this very well at all, I'm afraid. He's up there, now, in Virginia. Riding around, looking, talking to people. CNN had him on this morning. Did any of you see it?"

No one had seen it.

"Has anyone offered any kind of theory, any possible explanation?" asked Barbara.

"No. That's why I've come to you. When something happens... that is... something unusual..."

"What happened, Ms. Zarsa?"

"Yvonne, please, call me Yvonne,...I just want you all to know that I am not crazy. I know some people will think that, but I'm not...."

"Yvonne, what happened?"

"Phil was not really our child, ...biologically, I mean."

"We all knew that, your mother and me, I mean. Phil knew it. So what?" asked the aunt.

"What you don't know is, we didn't get him from an agency. I found him on a bus. In the bathroom, on the floor, a tiny infant. I was traveling alone, from our home in Norfolk to visit my husband. He was on assignment in Washington. It happened on the same highway exactly eighteen years ago last Friday, April 17.

94

FRAMED

"This is the last time I'm riding in this thing to Fayetteville until next winter. The AC on my ancient piece of junk works better than this one. Have you ever thought about getting this thing recharged, Ray?"

"It's not so easy anymore. Sorry, guys. I didn't know my wife was goin' to Raleigh until last night. She refuses to drive this old van anymore."

"I don't blame Gloria one bit. If I was her, I wouldn't lend you that brand new fancy Lincoln whether I was going anywhere or not."

"It's two years old, Harry."

"To me, that's new."

"It's really not all that hot today," said Tony West, the young man in the back.

Harry Miller drained the last of his Coors Lite and dropped the can in the bag with the other empty.

"Ray, can you stop at the Exxon in Mount Olive? I need a smoke and I need to make some room for another cold one."

"When was the last time we drove by this place without stoppin' on our way back from Fayetteville?" Ray answered as he slowed to make the turn.

"Tony, you sure you won't have one with me?" asked Harry.

"No, man. I will have a soft drink, though."

Ray Paramore rolled to a stop at the gas pump and got out to stretch and to refuel the eight-year-old Dodge van as his companions went inside the convenience store on the by-pass outside Mount Olive. In his early fifties, he was tall and slightly stooped. His dark hair was growing thin. He owed the thickness around his middle to too much North Carolina bar-be-cue and not enough exercise.

The unseasonably warm temperature had forced him to remove his jacket and loosen his tie, but it was warm, not hot, Ray thought. After all, it was only the first day of April. Everybody's got to have air conditioning twenty-four hours a day starting the minute it got to be seventy degrees. What's wrong with riding around with your windows down?

The three men were returning from a monthly district sales meeting for store managers for Blake Electronics Corporation. They all managed stores in eastern North Carolina. Ray and Harry were veterans who had been friends since Harry had moved to the area six years ago. Tony was a new manager who had trained under Harry for eighteen months before being assigned to manage a new store on the east side of Masonboro. He was slim, but athletic, African American, clean cut, handsome. He had recently married a science teacher at Masonboro Middle School.

Ray filled the tank on the van and went inside to pay. When he returned, he called to Tony.

"They have a call for you inside. It's urgent, they said."

Tony did not move.

"Go on. How could anyone call me here?"

96

"I don't know, but they asked for Tony West, who was ridin' with Ray Paramore."

Tony climbed out, perplexed. "This had better not be an April Fool trick, Ray. This had better not be an April Fool trick. And, you'd better not be gone when I get back."

He returned very quickly, grinning and pointing at Ray. Ray and Tony laughed.

"You are so easy," said Harry.

Ray pulled onto the highway, and Harry pulled another Coors Lite from a paper bag. Ray slowed to join a long line of vehicles waiting to pass a huge green tractor with a disc harrow folded up on both ends like the wings of a plane on an aircraft carrier. They were in farming country.

The tractor stopped on the broad green shoulder of the highway to allow traffic to pass.

"Tony, what do you think of the new DM?" Harry asked.

"He seems okay."

"Ray?"

"I think he'll be an even bigger asshole than Carey. If that's possible. At least Carey has a sense of humor."

"See there, Tony? When you've been around as long as we have, you'll be able to size up a new district manager in ten minutes. Mark my words, this guy'll be trouble."

"He says he wants ten percent gains every month," Ray went on. "We should check on his numbers up in Philadelphia."

"And he wants store managers to stay and close up every Friday and Saturday night," added Harry. "We're there anyway, but that needs to be our decision. I like to visit my old mother two or three weekends a year."

"You guys're getting me down," said Tony. "I was excited about my promotion, but you make me feel like I need to look for another line of work."

"Don't wait until you're our age. We don't have anywhere to go," said Ray. "They pick the biggest dickheads in the country with no experience dealing with people and no compassion for humankind whatsoever, give 'em a company car, and turn 'em loose on us. As if we don't get up and bust our ass every single day to make some money for ourselves and for the company."

Harry put his empty away and reached for another beer. Ray stopped behind a giant pumpkin-colored bus, and they watched two boys step down and make their way up their driveway, their shoulders sloped forward to support heavy loads of books on their backs. A third boy, much smaller, dashed past them to greet a long-haired dog that bounded around the corner of the house to meet him.

"And to top it all off, he had the audacity to tell a Bill Clinton joke. As if just because you're a BEC employee, you automatically despise the President of the United States."

"Greatest period of prosperity in the history of the nation. Those guys have made millions in the past eight years," added Ray. "The new DM'll get along fine with old dumbass Julian Flowers and some of our other right-wing colleagues."

"Like Mr. Smith and Wesson, Roger Barnes," said Harry.

"And don't forget the Reverend Mr. Davis," said Ray.

"The Neanderthal Club," said Harry.

"What in the world are you guys talkin' about?" asked Tony, laughing.

"Politics, my boy," explained Ray. "It seems that the right wing of the Republican Party has a foot-hold in good old Blake Electronics."

"Is that why Roger doesn't ride with you?" asked Tony.

"Do you want to sit and listen to that mindless bullshit for two hours?" asked Harry.

"No, but..."

"Where in the hell is he goin'?" Ray was referring to a highway patrol cruiser that blew past at a high rate of speed.

"How fast were you going?" asked Harry.

"I was doin' seventy."

"I'm glad your wife is a lawyer. Tony, old Raymond here never has to worry about any problems with law enforcement. If you get a ticket, just hand it to old Ray. His boss lady can take care of it. She's the hottest defense attorney east of Raleigh. And, she's up for a judgeship. Right, Ray?"

"Yeah."

"I'm impressed," said Tony. "What's her name?"

"Gloria Paramore."

"Gray, Paramore, and Wilson?"

"That's them."

"I've seen their ads," said Tony.

"Did you hide all her panties again this year?"

"No, but I put a little Vaseline on her door handle and under her steering wheel," said Ray.

"Tony, this guy enjoys April Fool more than anybody in the country."

"I noticed."

"Two years ago he ran an advertisement for a live-in maid for me for four thousand a month. I had to take the phone off the hook for a week," continued Harry. "One year he changed the sign in front of his uncle's convenience store to say 'Massage Parlor. Inquire Within.' ...What else, Ray?"

Tony laughed.

"One year I walked around the neighborhood early in the mornin' and taped up my friends' newspapers."

"You have a mean streak, Ray," laughed Tony.

"Uh-oh, we've got company."

Harry and Tony turned to see the flashing lights of a Barclay Police car that followed the old van as Ray guided it to a halt on shoulder of the four-lane bypass.

"Looks like we need to call Gloria after all," said Harry.

Two young officers emerged from the police car

99

and advanced on the van, one on each side. Ray opened the door and stepped to the ground, his wallet in hand.

"Good afternoon, Officer," he said.

Both policemen, in their late twenties, lean and wiry, wore dark uniforms. Each rested his hand on the butt of his pistol as he advanced toward the van. Ray was approached by an officer whose name tag read, "Carelli". Officer Carelli wore his auburn hair cut very short, a flattop. His face looked serious, almost angry. The second officer approached the van on the other side and peered in at Harry and Tony. Harry concealed his open beer can in the paper bag with the empties.

"May I see your license and registration, please?" asked Officer Carelli.

"Certainly, Officer," replied Ray. "May I ask why we were stopped?"

Carelli looked at Ray's license. "I'd like to see your vehicle registration, please," he said.

"Sure... Harry, would you see if you can find the registration card in the glove compartment? It's under the seat."

"Mr. Paramore, I clocked you at fifty-five miles per hour. The speed limit is forty-five. Were you watching your speedometer?"

"Joe, guess what he has in the glove compartment besides his registration card," called out the second officer.

Both policemen pulled their handguns and pointed them at the three passengers of the van.

"Step out of the vehicle, please, with your hands in the air. Move back to the police car. Put your hands on the car, and spread your feet."

"What is going on here?" asked Ray, as all three men moved toward the police car, hands in the air, as instructed.

The second officer checked the three for weapons then walked back to the van. When he returned, he held three small plastic bags containing what looked like marijuana and Harry's bag of three empty beer cans and one half full.

"The beer's ours, but I have no idea where the dope came from. I don't use it, and nobody I know does. I mean..."

"Sir, before you say anything, I'd like to advise you and the others of your rights."

While Carelli was on the radio calling for backup, a second police car rolled to a stop behind the first, and a short, blond policewoman emerged.

"You guys hit paydirt, I see," she said.

"Watch them, Hannah, please ma'am. We need to search the van."

"Tell them who your wife is," Harry whispered. "They can make this go away if they want to."

"Is that your pot?" Ray retorted.

"Hang on, gentlemen. They'll be right back," said Hannah.

Soon a stout young deputy sheriff in a brown uniform arrived. The sight of three law enforcement vehicles, blue lights whirling, slowed traffic in both directions to a near standstill as passersby craned to see what evildoers had been brought to justice.

Officer Carelli returned with two packages the size of two Philly steak-and-cheese subs. They were plastic bags filled with white powder.

"What in the hell is going on here?" asked Ray.

"I was going to ask you that very question, Sir," said Carelli.

"His wife is Gloria Paramore. She used to be the Assistant District Attorney over in Masonboro," said Harry.

"That should make this case very interesting," said the deputy.

Officer Carelli read the three prisoners their rights and they were handcuffed and loaded into the police cars. Ray sat in the back seat of the car driven by Hannah, whom he soon discovered had graduated from Masonboro High in the same class as his son, Edward.

"Eddie was one of the nicest boys in the class. And

one of the smartest. Did he marry...what was her name?"

"Samantha. No, they went their separate ways when they went to college"

"You have another son, a couple of years younger."

"George."

"George, ah yes. Does Eddie live around here?"

"No, he just graduated from UNC last year, and he's teaching at up in Arlington, Virginia ...Look, Officer, I never saw that stuff, whatever it is, before the policeman showed it to me."

"I know, you've said that. I believe you. We'll get to the bottom of this. Be patient. Are the cuffs too tight?"

"No, they're fine. I'm just so embarrassed. My wife will be humiliated."

"Eddie's not going to be too happy about it, either."

"You want to hear another ironic aspect of this thing? Your boss and I graduated from Masonboro High the same year."

"You're kidding. The chief? You look a lot younger than him. Maybe he can help you. On the other hand, he'll be under a lot of pressure not to show partiality."

"Thanks for the encouragement. Do you think the press has wind of this?"

"I'm afraid so. They all have scanners. I'm sorry this happened. You seem very nice."

"Thanks."

Ray was tired. He had been operating on a charge of adrenaline for some time. Now he was miserable and exhausted. He wanted to lie down and sleep. Maybe he would awaken to discover that this was a dream.

"What'll happen now?"

"You'll be booked and fingerprinted and arraigned before a magistrate who will set bail. You'll be released as soon as someone comes to post a bond for your bail."

"What about Harry and Tony?"

"The same. And they'll try to get each one of you to point a finger at the others. When it comes down to it, though, it's your car."

102

Hannah turned at the light and headed for the Barclay Police Station a few blocks away. People stopped to stare. He tried to turn away. He was certain that neither Tony nor Harry hid the drugs in his car. He felt ashamed that they had been arrested for riding with him. It had to be one of Gloria's enemies. Grace, their daughter, had driven the car several weeks ago while hers was in the shop. Could it have been a friend of hers? Not likely. Her friends were all at Chapel Hill.

Hannah parked at the rear of the station. Reporters ran to the car and began filming before Hannah opened his door. The deputy was there to assist her. The three of them moved rapidly though the gauntlet. Why were they laughing at him? Up the steps, through the heavy wooden doors. More photographers. There was Gloria...and Grace, his daughter, ...and the policeman with gray hair and mustache...it was the chief. They were all laughing. Harry and Tony turned and looked at him and laughed. His head spun. He looked up and caught sight of the banner. It read: "APRIL FOOL, RAYMOND PARAMORE. WE GOT YOU THIS TIME."

PASSIVE RESISTANCE

Sweat crept down Louis' neck in spite of the breeze that swept through the harbor. He spotted his ship, the *USS Chicago*, a half mile away, one of the many tall warships that lined the sides of the pier and loomed above him like the walls of some mountain canyon.

His suitcase had not seemed heavy when he lifted it from his bed the night before, but during the thirty-minute walk from the main gate, his clean underwear from home had turned to bricks, and he had switched hands several times.

The journey from back home had taken all day. It had been good to see his parents and family again, but he had decided that ten days in rural eastern North Carolina was about a week too long. It was good to be back in southern California, a hectic, irreverent place in an outrageous moment in history.

He stopped to watch the sailboats in the harbor, tiny white shapes on a lake of color, close enough to touch. He took a deep breath, picked up the bag, squared his shoulders, and continued.

The giant cranes in the distance were still, as were the trucks and trams that roared down the pier on workdays. No sailors, suspended from the main decks, were there to chip away at the copious layers of paint on the great gray hulls. Also missing were the civilian workers in blue jeans and steel-toed work shoes, smoking and drinking soft drinks and laughing beneath raised welding helmets, probably at the taxpayers who paid their salaries. It was Sunday. Only a trace of the smell of oil and paint and smoke lingered in the salt air.

The marine on guard duty snapped to attention as Louis approached the steps that led to the ship's brow. The young sentry didn't salute. Louis was in civies. He climbed the steps and lugged his suitcase across the narrow wooden walkway to the ship's main deck. The tide was in, and the steep climb to the deck of the ship was not an easy one. He paused at the halfway point and came to attention, facing the flag at the ship's stern. Then he turned to face the Officer of the Watch.

"Permission to come aboard, sir."

"Permission granted." The officer on the quarterdeck gave him an exaggerated salute and a broad smile. It was Louis' friend, Lieutenant junior grade Michael Burkhardt. Mike had been on duty when Louis reported aboard for the first time almost exactly one year before. He'd never forget that day. Louis was six-two, and when he stood at attention before Mike, Burkhardt's face and all above his Adam's apple loomed above the visor on Louis' cap. Burkhardt would have been an imposing figure, standing there in his spotless white uniform, but for his perpetual grin. He looked as if he had just heard a good joke and was planning to retell it.

"Welcome back, Lieutenant, j.g. Faulkner," he said as he offered his baseball glove-size hand.

"What are you talkin' about, Mike?"

"You made j.g. You and Maglio. Congratulations."

"Thanks."

Louis was no longer a lowly ensign. As the war in

105

Vietnam raged, the Navy had reduced the time to make j.g. from eighteen months to one year.

They shook hands. There was always energy in Burkhardt's grasp. His positive attitude and enthusiasm were contagious. Just being around him made Louis feel good. Mike was also one of a growing number of crew members, including Louis, that had doubts about whether the ship's mission was worthwhile.

"We have a departure date. Twenty-two August. Three weeks from tomorrow."

"So soon? Hellfire, we just got back from the last cruise," Louis said.

"I know. Deployed nine months, back home for four. Some of the married guys are sick about it."

They peered absently at the destroyer across the pier framed by the cloudless California sky.

"So, did you enjoy yourself down in shit-kicking country?" asked Burkhardt.

"Probably about as exciting as Scranton, Pennsylvania." Scranton was Burkhardt's home.

"Dull, huh?" Burkhardt grinned.

"I feel lucky to be back," Louis told him. "That was the worse flight I've ever had. We went through the thunderstorm to beat all thunderstorms. The lights went out. We fell hundreds of feet, several times. I thought the plane was coming apart. After we finally flew out of it, the sky turned bright red."

"Sounds like one of the amusement parks back home," he said.

"Anybody here that's goin' ashore tonight? Maglio or Wiesner around?"

"Maglio's over at the o' club, buying drinks. He said to tell you he picked up a set of silver bars for you when he bought his."

"What about Bobby?"

"Ah hurd Mr. Wiesner wuz in the brig, sur," said the young seaman who was standing watch with Lieutenant, j.g. Burkhardt. He was a short, slender figure with pale blue eyes. His starched white uniform and cap were spotless.

Burkhardt and Faulkner turned to face him, puzzled.

"Why?" Louis asked.

"I donno. AWOL, ah guess. Tha's awl ah hurd."

"Bullshit. Have you seen 'im, Mike?"

"No. I haven't seen him in a while. Everybody's on leave or in school. I don't see anybody. Where'd you hear that, Davis?"

"Ah don't even know. Wun o' th' boys."

"I'm going down below to see what I can find out," said Louis.

"Let me know, will you, Louis?"

"Will do, Mike."

On the deck below, Louis walked through the wardroom, a space large enough to seat the ship's one hundred officers and provide them with a place to relax. Four officers at a table studied their cards while another watched television from an easy chair. Lieutenant Commander Clark, the only black officer on board, played backgammon with Warrant Officer O'Brien, the ship's bo'sun.

"Commander, have you heard anything about Bobby Wiesner?" asked Louis.

Clark looked up and smiled. "No. What about him?"

"Nothing. Thank you, sir."

Louis stepped forward to the junior officers' bunkroom, stooping as he passed through the doorways. There he discovered two new ensigns that had reported aboard during his absence. None of the other officers were around. He introduced himself quickly and took his bag to his stateroom two doors down. There was no sign of Gould, his roommate.

Delighted to discover that there was hot water available, Louis showered quickly and put on his uniform. His white shoes were scuffed, but he stepped into them and headed aft to Bobby Wiesner's stateroom. It was vacant.

107

He switched on the light. The tiny gray cubicle with a bunk, a sink, a built-in writing desk, and a small closet, was bare. Louis felt strange.

He climbed the four flights of steps that led to the bridge. The wheel, the engine order telegraph, the gyro compass, and the leather captain's chair waited patiently in silence. He pushed open the door of the Combat Information Center, his principal workplace when they were underway. It was cold, a dark cavern. Several radar repeaters and other pieces of equipment lay open, their wiring hanging, works in progress. The red and green indicator lights around the space and the incessant drone of the air conditioner soothed the young man. He pulled a Winston from his shirt pocket and lit it.

Bobby Wiesner had been a veteran of one Westpac cruise when Louis, just out of Officer Candidate School, joined the ship in July, 1967. Louis had been assigned to the Operations Department, and Bobby had guided him through the learning process necessary for him to become a CIC Watch Officer. Wiesner was a bright, competent officer, but, like many of the junior officers, he was somewhat cynical. He had a good sense of humor, but he was not as popular among his shipmates as Louis was. Bobby was quiet, thoughtful, and somewhat aloof. He and Louis were the same age, twenty-four, but Bobby seemed older.

It must have been this quiet confidence that women found irresistible. He was over six feet, slim, upright. His hair was coal-black, and he had a long nose with slightly flaring nostrils and dark eyes that shone after he'd had several drinks. He was an agile dancer, and he attracted the most beautiful women whether the nightclub was in Los Angeles, Honolulu, or Hong Kong. He smoked non-filter cigarettes, the last person Louis knew who did so except for Louis' uncle, a farmer back in North Carolina.

He came from Buffalo, from a working-class family. His mother taught math at his high school. Bobby had graduated from Syracuse University, and his younger brother was a student there now. As the anti-war movement picked up steam on campus, little brother and his friends were giving Bobby a hard time about being in the military.

Louis returned to the main deck to find Burkhardt in the process of being relieved from duty. The two went below to Burkhardt's stateroom. He pulled two Cokes from his tiny refrigerator and handed one to Louis.

"I heard it costs ten thousand dollars for us to fire one round. We fired thirty-five hundred times in one week during the Tet Offensive," Burkhardt was saying.

"Maybe we should drop dollars instead of bombs. It would be cheaper," said Louis.

Burkhardt was required to remain on board during his section's twenty-four hours of duty. Louis decided to stay, also. After dinner they played poker with the Bo'sun and the two new ensigns.

The next morning Louis got dressed and sought out his immediate superior, Lieutenant James. James had spent sixteen years as an enlisted man before becoming an officer. He was a slim five-six, almost skinny. His large ears joined his closely cut head at right angles, and he wore black, horn-rimmed glasses. Louis found him having breakfast in the wardroom.

"Good mornin', Reggie."

"Well, well. Welcome back, Lieutenant, j.g. Congratulations. I guess you heard? You need to go ashore and get a set of silver bars."

"I got the eight-to-twelve watch."

"Somebody'll lend you some for today. How's North Carolina?"

"It's fine. Listen, Reggie, where's Bobby? I heard he was in trouble."

The lieutenant's face took on a serious expression. He pulled the younger man to him and lowered his voice.

"You don't need to tell anyone about this."

"Okay."

"When he got back off leave, he went to the

Captain and told him he wasn't going back to Vietnam. The Captain got on the horn and talked to some people. The next day, orders came through for him. He's assigned to a hospital ship. Bobby checked out the day his orders came in, last Wednesday."

NEED TO KNOW

Chapter One

The Dawsons stood at the port bow and waved to the fishermen, boat owners, and Southport dock workers as the Bald Head Island ferry slowly glided past the marina, the fishing docks, and the white clapboard waterfront restaurants. The festive atmosphere had infected everyone aboard, but the Dawson family may have been the most excited. As they entered the choppy blue-brown waters of the Cape Fear River, the vessel surged forward and swerved a few degrees to starboard. Male passengers, dressed in tee shirts and shorts, removed their caps, and women smiled from behind dark glasses as the moist breeze lifted their hair. Mothers clutched the small children in their laps. Dogs waited patiently at their masters' feet. The wind and the drone of the engine limited conversation on deck, but passengers clustered around the tables inside the air-conditioned cabin experienced no such restraints. The volume and pitch of their conversations reflected the holiday spirit in the air.

The vessel was crowded, as one would expect, because of the holiday, but no one seemed to mind. Calvin was not surprised that he and his family were the only African-Americans on board. That had been the case on their two previous trips to Bald Head Island. He watched out of the corner of his eye for stolen glances or other signs of disapproval. He had seen none. Upper middle-class white folks. They like us just fine as long as we behave like they do, he thought.

As if they had simultaneously received a signal from some unknown source, Frank and Sharon Dawson turned and smiled at their son. They were aware that Calvin was not as excited about spending a whole week in semi-isolation as his parents and his sisters were.

"We have a house this time," Frank had said, beseechingly, "You'll have your own room. No more pull-out sofa in the living room. You have your driver's license, now, and a golf cart comes with the house. You can drive that thing all over the island."

"They have cable. And we can rent movies at the grocery store," added Nicole, Calvin's twelve-year-old sister.

"And we can go swimming all day every day if we want to," Cynthia had reminded him. She was nine, but she thought she was much older.

"And Calvin, you might talk your dad into taking you to the club and giving you a chance to beat him again in tennis," added Mrs. Dawson.

Calvin had always been devoted to his family. He was not about to ruin it for them by telling them just how much he did not want to spend a week on an isolated island with no friends, no automobile, and no fast food. There was just one grocery store and two restaurants, a golf course, and the long, lonely, sandy beach. Moreover, Cynthia had become a real pain lately, and Calvin did not look forward to listening to her for a week. He was determined to make the best of things, however. His dad had spent a lot of money for their house, and all the others

112

had looked forward to the trip with such high expectations. Calvin would not spoil it for them.

Calvin's father, Frank, was a youthful, shorter-than-average forty-four-year-old. He was slender in build, quick, talented, a former band director. People felt comfortable around Frank Dawson. His friends knew him to be a man you could count on. The busy principal of a large high school, he adored his family, and he believed that they should spend time together. Three years younger than her husband, Sharon seemed to tower over him though she was taller by less than two inches. Relaxed, confident, she taught art at the university. She was soft-spoken, but her amber cat-eyes sent the message that her good-humored demeanor was not to be mistaken for faint-heartedness. Frank and Sharon were good parents, and if Calvin had to pretend a little to make them happy, he would do just that.

The slowing of the ferry signaled their approach to the harbor. On the left stood the landmark twin tower homes of the two architects who were among the first to build on the island. Palmetto trees and distinctive homes, the colors of blue, salmon, and beige ringed the rectangular harbor. Tin roofs reflected the morning sun, and Old Baldy, the nation's oldest lighthouse, loomed in the background. Calvin sensed that they were entering another world, one of mystery and enchantment, a sanctuary from all worries back home.

A large crowd waited at the ferry landing, some to greet the newcomers, others to board for the return to Southport. Deeply tanned crew members not much older than Calvin rushed about to secure the boat and roll the baggage containers down the gangplank to the claim area. The passengers disembarked to join the throng waiting under the massive roof of the train station-like landing. Frank and Cynthia hurried over for the keys while the others collected the bags. After a fifteen-minute tram ride through the maritime forest the Dawsons were deposited before a gray cedar-shake two-story home with white shutters, surrounded by ancient live oaks and towering palmettos. The girls ran from one room to another, marveling at the discovery of a modern kitchen, spacious family room, four bathrooms, and a large screened porch out back. They claimed the large bedroom in the rear that overlooked the marsh.

The next day, the Dawson family rose early and struck out for East Beach for the day. The crowd was the largest they had ever seen at a beach on Bald Head Island, but one could still walk a ways and find a private stretch of sand. Around noon they packed up and headed to the harbor for lunch. Calvin drove his parents in the golf cart and the girls preceded them on bicycles. Automobiles were not allowed on the island. A long line stood wrapped around the porch outside the restaurant, so the Dawsons decided to order sandwiches from the deli and eat on the deck overlooking the harbor. Their spirits were dampened, but only slightly, by the humid, almost motionless July air. Selecting a movie for the evening entertainment, they purchased a few groceries and headed for home.

Pivotal moments in history are sometimes recognized only in subsequent days, and the future hinges on small decisions that seem insignificant at the time. Such was the case when Calvin decided to walk home.

"In this heat? Don't be ridiculous," his mother said.

"It's probably three of four miles," said his father.

"I'll take the road through the golf course. It's shaded almost the whole way. I'll be fine. I need to stretch my legs."

"How long do you want them to be?" asked Nicole.

"Very funny. You all go on. I'll be fine."

And he was. Calvin loved long walks. He always had. It gave him a chance to think, to sort things out. Arms swinging, his long legs propelled him along in sweeping strides that altered their rhythm only to avoid oncoming golf carts. He returned the happy salutations of the golf cart passengers with brief waves and toothy grins. The narrow road took him though the shady interior of Bald Head

Island, heavily forested with a mixture of semi-tropical palmetto trees, live oaks, cedars, and undergrowth teeming with numerous species of animal life. Not only was it gorgeous, it smelled sweet and fresh, Calvin thought. The marsh came into view to his left, and he slowed to scan the scene. The sound of the place, the quiet, had a calming effect on him. He paused as he reached an abandoned golf cart that blocked the grassy median, and he waited for an approaching cart to pass. The deserted cart probably belonged to someone who had absentmindedly allowed the battery to run down. That was another thing Calvin liked about this place. Drivers left their carts beside the road or parked them outside the restaurant without concern about thieves. People here rarely locked their doors, and young girls wandered about after dark without fear.

Calvin glanced at his watch. He had been walking about thirty-five minutes. He estimated that he was about halfway home. He had to admit, his parents were right about the heat. He was drenched, and he was getting a little thirsty. He thought about the big glass of lemonade that he would enjoy when he got home. Then he would go for a swim in the ocean.

Then it happened. He heard the cart approaching from behind. It slowed and stopped, and, as he turned, a soft voice asked, "Do you need a ride?"

Later, they would laugh about Calvin's reaction when he saw the owner of the voice. He just stood there, jaw sagging, eyes wide.

"Was that your golf cart I passed?" she tried again.

Calvin attempted unsuccessfully to swallow. She was young, about his age, with a round face, turned-up nose, dark eyes, her teeth stark white against the darkest, silkiest skin he had ever seen. Her curly short hair accented her long neck. Her soft black shoulders were bare, and a light-colored halter covered most, but not all, of her full breasts. Her matching shorts were snug, and her long legs glistened in the reflected light. This was a cruel dream, a mirage, he thought. Only the white sneakers, one of which held the brake to the floor of the cart, seemed real.

The few seconds that it took for him to answer seemed like an embarrassingly long time. The girl smiled patiently.

"The cart?" Calvin muttered.

"The abandoned one I passed. It's not yours?"

"No. I don't know anything about it."

"So, you're just out for a walk. Don't get too hot." She released the brake.

"Wait! I'm hot. I mean, yes, I need a ride. Please."

He stood there.

"Get in. Out of the sun."

Finally, Calvin hurried around the cart and leaped, landing on the seat hard enough to bounce the cart.

"I'm Candice Brock."

Calvin took the moist hand that she offered and watched a bead of perspiration make its way down the side of her neck.

"I'm Calvin Dawson."

She looked good, sounded good, and felt good, and, as he expected, she smelled like some tropical wild-flower.

"Where do you live?"

"Barclay. North Carolina."

"No, I mean where are you staying? Where can I drop you off?"

"I'm not really going anywhere in particular. Where were you headed?"

"Just out riding. Maybe go for a walk on the beach."

"Do you mind if I join you?"

"Of course not. When did you arrive, and how long will you be staying?"

"We got here yesterday for one fun-filled week in paradise."

"You don't like it here?" she asked.

"Of course I do. There's just not much to do. How

116

about you? I mean, are you here with your family?"

"My mom and dad. My sister's in Europe. We'll be leaving Thursday morning."

She turned right on Muscadine Wynd and they headed south, winding their way under the shaded canopy, toward the ocean.

"Where are you from?" he asked.

"Charlotte."

"My cousin is a junior at UNC-Charlotte."

"How about you?"

"I'm still in high school. I'll be a senior."

"Me too. Do you really want to walk on the beach?"

"Sure. If you do."

"It's still so hot. Let's go back to the harbor and get something cold to drink."

"Okay."

The turned right and they headed west along beach road.

"You sure are agreeable. You must not like it here because you miss your girl friend back in Barclay."

"No. I don't have anyone special." He lied. He and Melissa had been going together for over a year. Now he thought it was only because neither had found anyone they liked better.

"How about you?"

"Robert and I broke up last May. I've been waiting for someone like you to come along."

Calvin spun around to stare at her laughing face. Yes, he had heard correctly. And there he sat with his mouth hanging open once again.

Chapter Two

"You guys ready?"

"I need a shower. Let's have one more first," replied Henry Sanderson. The lanky lad of eighteen seated at the end of a large oak table studied his cards.

"That's what I mean, birdbrain." The speaker was

Graham Warf, Henry's cousin and closest friend, also eighteen. Graham was a ruggedly handsome young man, broad-shouldered and formidable. He wore his sandy hair close, and his somber expression and reserved manner led many observers to mistake him for a man much older.

A reddish brown mane with a life of its own sur- rounded Henry's beet-red face. He wore his hair long in order to hide his ears, which owed their prominence not so much to their size as to the right angle from which they protruded from his head. His lopsided grin and glistening eyes indicated that the beer in his hand was not his first.

"Alexis?"

"Not quite. I'm still working on this one. I'm going to the loo, as they say in the old English movies. Don't do anything fun until I get back."

Alexis was Henry's older sister, a college girl.

"It's impossible to have fun when you're not around. Hurry back," replied Graham.

"Heads up, son," he said to Henry as he turned.

The refrigerator door swung open and ejected a frosty green bottle of Rolling Rock that sailed across the room to be snagged by Henry, who twisted off the cap and tossed it toward the garbage can. A second bottle followed the first until it veered to the left and circled the room twice, finally settling gently on the table before Graham's massive frame. Graham, unlike his cousin, watched the cap as it twisted free from the bottle and sailed away to the trash. Graham's special gift was a big deal, Henry was thinking, but we see it so much we don't think any more about it than shooting a thirty foot jump shot or running four or five balls on the pool table. Unearthly tricks and magical feats performed by Graham each day had become a normal part of their lives. Henry couldn't remember not being conscious that there was something very strange about his cousin.

Henry remembered falling out of a tall tree when he was very young. Silently he had said goodbye to the world on his way down. Instead he tumbled softly into the grass

118

below. Graham said, "I stopped you." But Henry didn't
know what he meant.

Then in the second grade, a fourth grader was
picking on Alexis. Suddenly the big bully began to fall
down. Each time he struggled to get to his feet, he fell.
Finally he gave up and lay on the ground in a prone position, sobbing. Graham stood there watching him.

Then there was baseball. Graham could throw a
wicked curve at a very early age. He could make it change
speeds and rise or drop. No one could hit the ball when he
pitched for his little league team. Also, he could send a
basketball through the hoop from any angle from the back
court. And kick a football through the uprights from fifty
yards out.

But Graham was reluctant to show off his gift. He
did so only in the company of those he trusted, and he
trusted only his cousins, Alexis and Henry. Of course,
Graham's mother knew his secret. And eventually Henry's
parents and younger sister found out. Anne Sanderson and
Janice Warf, mothers of Henry and Graham, were sisters,
and Henry was sure that their brothers, his uncles, must
know. But conversation, private or otherwise, about
Graham's gift was taboo.

This instinctive desire to keep his gift a secret re-
sulted in Graham's decision to give up sports, a decision
that bewildered and disappointed his coaches. They wanted
to know why Graham, at six-six and two-twenty and one of
the best athletes to come along in a long time, refused to
do his part for the glory of Masonboro High's athletic
program. It was cheating, he explained privately, to use his
gift, and he didn't believe that he could play and resist
using these skills. Henry didn't agree with his decision, but
he understood it. Graham was so competitive. He had a
talent for making things happen. Once in a while they went
out and won money from some arrogant pool shark. One
night they won three thousand dollars. The next day
Graham gave it to the Salvation Army.

They had some fun with the gift at times. At

119

Masonboro High School basketball games, Graham sat in the bleachers and guided Eddie Baldwin's shots to the basket. Eddie wasn't really that good a player, but he played hard and became a favorite of the crowd. He scored twenty-four points in the loss to Greenville Rose.

But most of the time Graham considered his gift a curse. He was a personable young man who made friends easily but kept to himself. His only real friend was Henry. They had been inseparable since infancy. Alexis was a sometime third in their inner circle.

"Well, are you high school boys ready to take me out and help me find a real man?" Alexis had changed to her fourth outfit of the day. This time she wore a dark blouse and pants combination with short heels that would be more appropriate for a nightclub in the city than for the informal beach pubs that they would be visiting. Alexis' long, shapely legs and slim figure turned men's heads wherever she went. She had cut her dark hair short for the summer, and her long neck and face were reddish-brown from their day in the sun. Her long Sanderson nose and thin lips tended to give her face a stern, sad look, except when she smiled. And she wore her sly, disarming smile most of the time. Valedictorian of her high school class and now an honors student at UNC in Chapel Hill, Alexis had a quick wit and a charm that attracted people wherever she went. She enjoyed spending time with her hard-headed brother and their cousin, a second brother, really, but she harbored a twinge of jealousy of the relationship they shared. She was a member of their inner circle, but she didn't feel equal.

She had agreed to spend four days at the family house at Atlantic Beach with the two boys because they would be off the following week to Quantico, Virginia. The two were scheduled to report for six weeks of training for some secret career in the military. It had to do with Graham's gift. Henry was a part of it because Graham wouldn't go without him. She wanted to go, also, but she admitted she would probably refuse if they offered her the chance. The military was not in her plans for her future.

The trio was seated at one end of the massive wooden table on the upper level of the beach house. Windows on three sides provided light that created a cheerful atmosphere during the day and allowed the sea breeze to sweep though the house at night. The three had arrived from Masonboro late on the afternoon of the previous day. After a seafood dinner at their favorite restaurant on the Morehead City waterfront, they checked out the nightlife in the area. The next morning, Alexis, anxious to show off her newly-acquired sailing skills, had insisted that they rent a boat, and they spent the day exploring the islands east and north of Atlantic Beach. Sailing out past Fort Macon and along the length of Shackelford Banks, the ancient island home of a herd of wild ponies, they tied up at the small dock at Cape Lookout. After an inspection of the lighthouse and museum, they set out on a trek along the lonely coast of Core Banks. Only birds and marine wildlife and a few fishermen whose families had lived there for decades inhabited the island. The trio trudged along in silence most of the way, cooling their feet in the surf and inhaling the salty air.

But they hadn't brought enough food, and the beer ran out, so they sailed back to Morehead City for another hearty meal before returning to the family vacation home on the third row from the ocean. They played hearts at the kitchen table as they had done since childhood, and no one was surprised when Alexis won.

"Maybe your friend with the beard and missing teeth will be back tonight," said Henry.

"I like the short one with the pony tail and tattoo," Alexis retorted. Suddenly she felt her pants sliding down her hips. When she glanced at their cousin, sure enough, he had that funny, out-of-this-world look that he took on whenever he was up to one of his magic tricks.

"Graham, you son of a bitch!"

She charged her cousin, armed with a pillow from the sofa in her right hand, the waistband of her pants in her left. She hammered away at his arms that shielded his blond crew cut and laughing sun-burned face until she broke though and landed a satisfying blow to his left ear. Graham fell to the floor, and his foot tipped Henry's chair backward. Henry lay where he landed for several seconds, his long bare feet pointing skyward like a set of water skis poised for action. All three laughed for a long time, and, when Henry rose from the floor to reveal shorts and tee shirt soaked in beer, the laughter resumed.

Chapter Three

Calvin stood at the dock and waved as the ferry's horn sounded its departure. Candice returned his wave vigorously, her crisp white open-collar shirt and shorts in sharp contrast to her skin, dark in the shade of the canopy of the upper deck. A truly graceful young lady, Calvin thought, and he wondered why she seemed so happy. He was disappointed that she was not crying. He was miserable. They had been together for three glorious days, and now he had to face the next three here on the island without her.

"Can I come to Charlotte next week?" he had asked the day before.

"I wish I would be there. I'm leaving for France on Sunday to visit my mother's sister. I'll be there for a month. You can come in the fall."

"Is your aunt on line? They have the Internet in Europe, you know."

"I really don't know. If not, I'll still write." As she answered, she leaned into him and kissed him. Then she stood up.

"We need to go. They'll be out searching for us."

They had been sitting on a blanket at the southernmost point of East Beach, fertile fishing grounds for pelicans, dolphins, and many other species, including several young men who had been casting into the surf all afternoon. The breeze and its smell and the angle of the sun, low in the west, cast a spell that made standing and collecting their belongings a difficult task for Calvin. The forty-five minute walk to Candice's parents' beach house would be their final opportunity for privacy for a long time. Even so, they marched in silence most of the way.

"Candice, why do your parents want to send you so far away for college?"

"They just want the best for me. Just like yours. Didn't your dad mention MIT and Cal Tech the other day?"

"Yeah, but he knows that I can stay right here and receive an excellent education at Duke."

Both were lost in their thoughts for a few minutes. Then Calvin spoke. "Did you ever consider attending a traditionally black college?"

"Absolutely. When I was younger, Mom talked about my following in her footsteps to North Carolina Central. Dad graduated from A&T, and his sister went to Fayetteville State. I thought about Howard University at one time."

"What made them change their minds?"

"I don't know. I guess they sense that times have changed. They know I'm bright and I can succeed at a top school and the opportunities for minorities and women are unlimited. So why not?"

"Where in the hell is Bryn Mawr, anyway?"

"Pennsylvania."

"Why there?"

"That was just one of several possibilities. I wanted an all-girls school. I guess I just want to eliminate a lot of competition to raise my odds for success."

They lapsed into another brief period of silence. Gazing into the setting sun, she said, "This is breath-taking."

She reached for him, and he leaned over to kiss her. As they continued they held one another, an embrace made slightly awkward by the fact that the level of her eyes met that of his armpit, each pretending not to notice.

"I'm going to miss you, Calvin."

Chapter Four

"Mr. Michelangelo, welcome back. Did you have a productive summer?"

Arthur Sanderson forced the door to his storage space closed and turned to greet his principal and longtime friend, Frank Dawson. They shook hands.

"Hello, Frank. Yeah, I did a little painting. I spent most of it painting the inside of the house."

Frank was making the rounds, visiting with returning teachers and helping the new ones get settled in. AD Murphy was a large school, the only high school inside the city limits of Barclay. There were ninety-eight full time teachers and three part timers and more than fifty other staff members. Art, like his co-workers, trusted Frank Dawson and enjoyed working for him.

"Say, I heard you finally spent some of that pile of money you've been hoarding," said Art.

"What? Oh, the house at Bald Head? Yeah, I went and jumped in the deep end, I guess."

"I'm jealous. Its beautiful down there."

"Well, it's payback time, Mr. Sanderson. You and Anne just let us know when you can come. We've been in your debt for years for all those good times we had at your place at Atlantic Beach."

"Well, you were invited a lot more than you came. And you always brought the whiskey. But I am looking forward to seeing your place. I know you're all excited about it."

"Yep, we are. Even Calvin."

"And what has my main man decided to do with his life next year?"

"He's going to apply at several places. A lot depends on scholarships."

"That kid has a world of talent. He can do whatever he wants to."

"Thanks. What about Henry? He graduated from

Masonboro last spring, didn't he? Is he still planning to attend N.C. State?"

"That's right. He and his cousin are due in Saturday from summer camp in Quantico. Both of them have some kind of Department of Defense scholarship."

"Nice. How about Alexis? Still at UNC?"

"Yep. She'll be a junior. Three-six average."

"Outstanding. And the baby?"

"Greta. She's in the tenth grade."

"That is hard to believe."

"She's tall, like her mother. And just as hard-headed. How are your girls?"

"Grown. Both of them. At nine and twelve. And they want to move to Bald Head permanently."

"I'm looking forward to teaching Calvin one more year. Is he still leaning toward MIT?"

"He's still going around in circles. I truly believe that he would like to go somewhere and pursue his art. We are indebted to you for helping him to develop his talent. Oh, I don't know how to advise the boy. He loves his math and he loves his computers, too. I guess it'll come down to what kind of scholarships he gets."

"Well, Frank, that's not too bad a problem to have. Calvin will excel no matter what he chooses."

Arthur had been the art teacher at AD Murphy High since he transferred from the middle school fourteen years before. Frank Dawson had become the principal two years later, and the two quickly became friends. Arthur had driven the twenty-two miles from Masonboro every day since then primarily because of his friendship with his principal. Frank backed the art program. Art got whatever he wanted, and Art delivered. Murphy High art students had won awards and been recognized throughout the state. Art was a terrific teacher and a fine artist, and Frank wanted to keep him. After all, he didn't know any other school that had Art teaching art.

"Did you say Henry was due in from some kind of camp? What kind of outfit has he joined?"

125

"I don't know what to say, Frank. He and his cousin are in a special program for FBI agents or some other government program, paramilitary or something. I really don't know. It's a big secret."

"When are they getting in?"

"Due in tomorrow night. Flying in to Masonboro."

"And they have scholarships to State?"

"Yeah, Uncle Sam's paying for it. Tuition, room and board, and books. Even spending money."

"Can't beat that."

Frank wanted to ask more about the strange good fortune of young Mr. Sanderson, but he could see that the subject made Art nervous. Instead, he glanced at his watch.

"Hey, I have a meeting downtown in a few minutes. You have a shipment of supplies in the office. You know Ms. Cannon. She likes to get it out of there as soon as possible. I'll see you later."

"Will do. Adios."

As Art the Art Teacher returned to his task of cleaning his room, his thoughts returned to his son. What in the heck was his Henry involved in? Damn that Graham Warf. Why couldn't he take his magic powers to the army or CIA or somebody and leave Henry alone?

Arthur Sanderson's three children came first in his life. He had been born and raised a few miles from Masonboro on a tobacco farm, the youngest of five. When he went off to Carolina to study English and then to follow his older brother to law school, he was determined never to return to quiet, conservative, churchified eastern North Carolina. Then his brother was killed in Vietnam.

His oldest brother had avoided the draft by teaching school for six years. Another had joined the navy and gone to OCS to become an officer and a gentleman. But Kenny, the third son, had dropped out of NC State and joined the Army. He was flying a helicopter, evacuating the wounded, when he was shot down. His body had arrived in a sealed coffin one week before Christmas, 1969. The

126

family had been devastated. Art's father quit farming and took on strange behavior such as wandering though the woods for hours at the time. Art's mother stopped going to church for three years. She spent a lot of her time in bed. Art's sister, a sophomore on a full scholarship to Duke, quit school and hitchhiked to California. Arthur attended Carolina for one semester and followed his sister to the west coast. They shared a rundown house in Newport Beach with three members of a rock band, one of which was his sister's boy friend.

The time that the farm girl and her little brother spent in wild and wooley Southern California, the out-rageous years of 1970 and 1971, tested them, but it didn't get the best of them. The lifestyle of round-the -clock music and drugs and casual sex, the aspiring artists, actors, and models, the camaraderie and good cheer, and the collective optimism created an exciting atmosphere that changed their lives.

Neither of the two suffered negative effects from their experiences. In fact, it was during this period that Arthur discovered painting. When he did, he knew exactly what the rest of his life held for him. Returning to Chapel Hill in the fall of 1972, Art changed his major to art, and he spent the next twenty-six years pouring his ideas and dreams onto his canvases. During his junior year he had met Anne, a delectable young freshman from Silver Spring, Maryland, whose family had moved to Raleigh the year before. They were married three years later, and unlike most of their friends, they had remained that way. Arthur had taken a job teaching in order to make ends meet, but he soon discovered his second passion, or third if you include his wife: teaching young people about art. Now he had arrived. He had sold his last three pieces of work for more than he made teaching for an entire year. Yet he had never seriously considered giving up his classroom. He loved art, and he loved his students. To him, life couldn't be better. Until now. Arthur and Anne were loving parents, good parents. Firm but caring. Their children had always been good girls and boys. Creative children. Top of their classes, popular, active in school activities.

But now, they were becoming adults. That was a different ball game. Mom and Dad hadn't quite learned to handle it.

Chapter Five

"Hit the deck, you maggots! Rise and shine!"

Graham Warf had returned from breakfast and his eight o'clock calculus class.

Henry groaned. Graham's return to the room meant that he had forty minutes to dress and make the fifteen-minute walk to his ten o'clock class. What time did they get in last night? How did Graham do it? No matter how late they stayed out, he was always fresh as spring rain, never missing his eight o'clock classes. Henry turned back over and covered his head with a pillow, but the foot of his bed suddenly rose two feet into the air, paused for a few seconds, then dropped abruptly to the floor with a thunderous thud that shook the room.

"Okay, okay, I'm getting up. Damn, man. Somebody's going to walk in one day when you're doing one of your tricks. Then you'll have a lot of questions to answer."

"Nobody's coming in here this time of day."

"Alright. You know what McMann said."

"My man, McMann. My main spook. You worry too much. We're only young once."

"What has being young got to do with jumping off a tenth floor balcony?" Henry asked.

The pair chuckled as they shared the memory of the previous evening. After a night on the town with two guys who had returned to their room down the hall, Graham succumbed to the urge to entertain his cousin by jumping off the balcony of the tenth floor of Sullivan Dormitory, not once but three times. On the second leap, he did a swan dive, and on the third he drew himself into a ball and flipped three times before landing on his feet as softly as if he had been jumping off the kitchen table.

It was the first week in November. The cousins from Masonboro were in their freshman year at NC State University in Raleigh. Both were serious students who attended classes regularly and completed all assignments, but they found concentration difficult after their summer at the military training facility in Quantico. They had participated in a program that was custom designed for them, all because the government wanted to harness Graham's power. Graham needed a companion, and Graham insisted that his cousin and long-time confidant be the man at his side.

Chapter Six

Graham Warf, the only offspring of David and Janice Warf, weighed more than forty pounds when they adopted him at eighteen months of age, and he didn't stop growing until his seventeenth year. David, a New Yorker who came south with the local pharmaceutical company, had been diagnosed with Lou Gehrig's Disease when Graham was twelve. He died when his son was fifteen. Janice, the older sister of Anne Sanderson, ran a dress shop in a fashionable shopping center.

As a student at Meredith College in Raleigh in the early seventies, Janice took a part time job at the city's largest department store in order to get out of the dormitory. She had been working in women's clothing since that time. Janice's success was due to her willingness to work long hours in a business that she loved. She had an eye for innovative designs, and she was adept at picking items that her customers were willing to pay top prices for. She had made many friends in the garment industry over the years, but, unlike her younger sisters, Janice was never considered an attractive woman. Tall and slightly stooped, large-boned, and blond, she was apparently destined to be an old maid until Walsch

Pharmaceutical came south bringing David Warf with them. He had rented the other apartment in her duplex. Within two years they were married. Both wanted a child, and when they discovered that they could not produce one of their own, they applied for adoption at several agencies and waited. Within a year they were rewarded with a beautiful eighteen-month-old boy. They were so excited and happy that neither parent made a serious effort to obtain information about the boy's parents. They knew only that he was the son of a single mother who had died of cancer.

Janice doted on her son, and when she discovered his gift, she considered it a curse and did her best to keep it a secret. It was simply one more obstacle in a lifetime of adversity.

Janice was grateful to Anne for allowing Graham to spend so much time at the Sanderson household. The sisters had always considered Henry and Graham to be positive influences on each other. The boys brought home good grades and finished high school second and third in their class, and no one seemed to remember who was second and who was third. Henry was the star of the English department, winning several creative writing awards and writing and directing a play his senior year. Graham excelled in science. He was fascinated by both chemistry and physics, and he took evening classes at the university during his senior year in high school. Henry had served as president of their sophomore and junior classes, and Graham was president of the National Honor Society during their senior year. Both had starred on the Quiz Bowl team.

The pair did not neglect their social life, however. When they arrived at a nightclub or party, people turned to stare at Graham's handsome, towering figure. Graham was an excellent dancer. He enjoyed dancing almost as much as drinking beer.

Henry was three inches shorter than his cousin. Long and lean and just a little clumsy, he was a favorite among his classmates. Henry enjoyed being the center of

130

attention, and he liked meeting new people and making new friends. He had a gift for listening to people talk about themselves and for finding good in everyone. He drew stories and jokes from a well-known collection he carried in his head. Graham said Henry could sell airline tickets to a bald eagle.

The boys' friends were all ages and all races. If a small vestige of racial tension lingered in Masonboro after all these years, and most people believed that it did, Henry and Graham were not conscious of it. They grew up in families that defended and befriended African-Americans, and Henry and Graham were at their best at a nightclub where they were the only Caucasians in the crowd.

Anne Sanderson was as proud of her nephew as she was of her own children. She had added a few pounds in the right places during twenty-two years of marriage and childbearing, but Anne was as pretty at forty-three as she had been on her wedding day. She wore her long red hair in various fashionable styles and dressed in the latest and smartest from New York's garment district. She was the eighth grade guidance counselor at Masonboro's largest middle school, and she set a standard that made the faculty there among the best dressed in the county.

But Anne didn't feel beautiful. She felt tired. She had enrolled in graduate school the year Greta, the baby, entered four-year-old kindergarten. Two years later she took the job as a counselor, and she had since been juggling the demands of work with scout meetings, band concerts, little league games, piano lessons, and dozens of orthodontist appointments, not to mention visits to the bedside of her invalid mother.

Anne had not minded having Graham around all these years. In fact, she felt that Alexis, Henry, and Graham had turned out so well due more to their influence on each other than from that of her or of her husband, Mr. Art-man. And they had certainly set good examples for Greta, whose grades were at the top of her class.

Anne was glad that she was able to help her older

sister in some way. Janice had always been there when Anne needed her. There was Janice's house at Atlantic Beach, always available for use as if it were theirs. Not to mention the clothes, thousands of dollars worth over the years which Anne bought at wholesale prices. Anne wished that her sister were not so lonely, and she felt guilty that she was glad, in a way, that David was gone. The Warf's marriage had never been a smooth one, and Anne suspected at times that Janice had covered for David and that things were worse than they appeared. Then came the period of illness that held Janice and her son hostage for three long years. Thank goodness for the Walsch medical insurance.

The sisters almost never spoke of Graham's gift. Anne was curious, but Janice was reluctant to discuss it. The older sister made it clear that her son's power was just another physical trait, like Henry's ears or Graham's size, or Anne's and Greta's red hair. She had been partially successful in preventing Graham from using his gift with a combination of persuasion and coercion, and now, for the most part, she just didn't think about it.

Neither Janice nor Anne knew what to think of the mysterious government program that had seduced their sons and that was paying for the boys' education, not four years but seven. Janice had called their congresswoman who replied by mail a week later:

"Dear Ms. Warf:

"Thank you for your call. It is always a pleasure to serve one of my staunchest supporters. Thank you for all your help over the years.

"I understand your concern for your son and for your sister's son, but, frankly, I was surprised to discover how little information is available about the program in which they are enrolled. After several attempts, I called and spoke to the Deputy Attorney General. He assured me that your son and nephew are enrolled in a special pilot program

for high school graduates that is sponsored by the Marines in cooperation with the FBI. He said that training for the young men is being handled by a panel of elite FBI agents. Furthermore, he assured me that the training is not harsh and that the boys are as safe at the training camp than they would be at home in bed. More details will be released as their training progresses and as the Bureau has an opportunity to evaluate their performance.

"I hope this news puts your mind at rest. When you hear from the young men, please extend an invitation from me for them to visit my office in Washington.

"Please contact me if I can be of more service.

Yours truly,
Nora Franklin"

Chapter Seven

Henry Sanderson had run four balls and was drawing a bead on the eight when his cousin strode through the door of the student center. They met there for lunch at one on Monday, Wednesday, and Friday. Henry sometimes shot a few games of pool with whomever was hanging around as he waited. Today it was a sophomore from High Point. He wasn't very good.

"Mail call, Slick. I've got something hot for you. I'm tempted to hold it until after your two o'clock class 'cause lover boy, you won't be worth a doughnut hole after you read this."

He handed his cousin a pink envelope. Henry held his breath as he read the return address and retired to one of the seats that lined the wall to pour over the scented handwritten pages. Graham picked up the abandoned stick and shot the eight ball. The black ball ricocheted around the table, stopped before the corner pocket, then rolled slowly in.

"You want to play another?" asked Graham.

"No, thanks. I've got a class. See you around,"

answered the sophomore from High Point as he quickly hung up his stick and grabbed his coat.

"Man, it's getting harder and harder to amaze people. It's the special effects in the movies. They don't know the difference between real life and make believe."

Henry didn't answer.

"What does she want, stud? She want you to come running to St. Louis for some loving? I thought she would've found one of those rich brewery owners by now."

Henry wasn't listening. The letter was from Rachel Bloom, the girl Henry had dated all summer, the one to whom he had written three times before finally receiving the four-page reply that he held in his hand. Rachel and her identical twin, Lisa, were training along with Henry and Graham. They were sophomores at Washington University in St. Louis. Like Graham, they had a gift that was of great interest to the government. They could communicate telepathically.

The training program included physical training with Marine officer candidates, firearm training and introduction to counterespionage with FBI recruits, and various classes dealing with the organization of the Departments of Defense and Justice. The boys from North Carolina and the Bloom sisters from Long Island scored near the top of all their classes. Their presence was the subject of whispered conversations among instructors and fellow students. Only their manager, Colonel McMann, his assistant, Captain Carla Lowe, and a small number of high-ranking members of the intelligence community knew all the details. The four trainees had discussed their situation throughout the summer.

"How much of this abuse do the regular military people get and how much is just for us freaks?" Lisa Bloom asked without expecting an answer.

"Or just spook trainees?" Graham added.

"They're claiming that we're the first. Who are they kidding?" Henry laughed. He laughed a lot around the Bloom sisters.

134

"We don't even know if we are the only four. For all we know, they could have programs like ours all over the country," Rachel joined in.

"That's the nature of the spy business," said Graham. He liked the idea of being a spy. John LeCarre was his favorite author.

"Have you guys gotten any more out of McMann on what they will expect when we graduate?"

"He just says read the contract. I told him we needed a whole covey of lawyers to tell us what that thing says."

"Covey?"

"Herd, city girl, flock. I'm not even sure why I'm here at all. I don't have any super powers," said Henry.

At first, the contrast in the Carolina accent and that of New York was a topic of interest that provided an opportunity for great imitations by both sides. By the third week nobody noticed anymore.

"Has anybody considered that seven years of college with all this fun every summer might get old?"

"We can all do whatever it takes. What kind of toothpaste do you ladies use?" Henry wanted to know.

"Will you stop with the teeth, Henry," Rachel was smiling. "You'll make us keep our mouths shut forever."

"Promises, promises." said Graham.

"No, Rachel, I don't mind if he admires our pearly white teeth. I just want to know what else he likes."

Lisa enjoyed teasing Henry. In fact, she liked to tease everyone she met. Henry wondered if she talked that way to her famous rock star boy friend back home that she bragged about. He decided that she probably did.

"Well, there's those deep dark eyes that sparkle when you're happy and turn red when you get angry, which is most of the time."

"Henry, you haven't seen us angry. You just wait," said Lisa.

"I also like what I see when you're walking away. Or better yet, running."

"And those stubby little legs," added Graham.

"Stay out of this, Lieutenant Warf. We are a respectable five feet four. Its you two who are the mutants. Is that what grits and black-eyed peas do for you, grow you into giant behemoths, tall as those pine trees back home?" Lisa laughed.

"It was the collards and corn bread. And an active sex life," retorted Lieutenant Warf. That had been his handle for years. It was a reference to Captain Picard's security officer aboard the starship *Enterprise*. Lieutenant Worf was also a large individual.

"One of these days you two can come to New York and have some matzo ball soup," Rachel suggested.

And now she wanted Henry to come to New York during the holiday break. Graham was invited, also. They could stay at Aaron's place. Aaron was Lisa's boy friend, the musician. Henry was relieved to hear from Rachel. She wrote that she had not answered his first two letters because she had been so busy. She was taking some difficult courses this semester. Henry thought that Washington University must be rough if the twins found it difficult. They each had to read only half of the material and exchange information. They were in for a shock if one had to take a course without the other. The Bloom twins' gift was truly amazing. Henry and Graham had assisted in some of the experiments conducted by Colonel McMann. Isolated from each other in sound-proof rooms, Henry could dictate messages to Rachel which Lisa wrote on a pad in the other room. In another, one sister watched a training tape and the other answered the test questions. In still another, one sister drew the symbols that the other observed on a screen. No one knew where this gift had come from nor what practical use it would have.

The sisters, referred to by male trainees as "the Bloomers", were somewhat short and tending toward stout but in excellent physical condition due to a lifelong dedication to exercise and a healthy diet. Their jet-black hair was cut short, almost like a man's, and their milk-white complexions had turned to creamy tan. Their noses were slightly turned up, and their lips were full, ready to burst into a broad smile at the slightest excuse. They were intelligent and full of energy, eager to try new experiences. Henry had fallen in love with Rachel, the one who didn't already have a boy friend.

Chapter Eight

"Cal!"

Calvin Dawson shared a table with his new girl friend and a dozen of their cronies at their favorite spot in the AJ Murphy High School cafeteria.

"Cal!"

Calvin turned and waved at Tommy Bowen who was calling his name.

"Yeah, Tommy, over here!"

"The principal wants to see you. Right away."

Tommy glanced around to see if anyone appreciated his humor. A few people obliged with a chuckle.

"Okay, Tommy. Thanks. I'll be right back, Meca."

He stood up and headed for his father's office.

"Good luck, Calvin. You'll need it."

"I knew he'd catch you sooner or later."

Dozens of people spoke to the tall young man as he made his way through the cafeteria and the lobby. Everyone knew Calvin, the principal's son, president of the student body, top of his class, and one of the friendliest people at the school.

"What's up, Daddio?" Calvin asked when he reached his father's office.

"Calvin, come in and have a seat, son."

Calvin sat down.

"Calvin, how long did you think you could keep it from me?"

"Aw, Dad, cut the bullshit. I thought something was wrong. What is it?"

"Just a letter, my boy. From the NC State School of Design. I wanted to know what they have to say."

"Thanks, me too." He tore into the envelope and read.

"I got it. Full scholarship."

Frank Dawson read the letter and held out his hand to grab his son. The two embraced.

"I'm proud of you, my man. One down and two to go. What happens if you get the one from MIT and the one from Georgia Tech?"

"Well, I'm glad I got this one because I've been wanting to talk to you. I know you've wanted me to be an Ivy League man of the world."

"You've got the talent and the grades to go any-where. You need the contacts you'll make at the top schools if you are going to be our first black president."

"Well, at the risk of bein' a big disappointment to you, I've decided I don't want to live in Boston or Atlanta or New York. I want to come home on the weekends and be with you guys. I want to be with people from North Carolina."

"Think about it some more. We'll talk about it. You make your own decision. Don't ever do something you don't want to just to please me."

"Thanks, Dad. I've got English right now. Talk to you tonight. Thanks for calling me down."

"Want me to call your mom? You want to tell her when you get home?"

"You can call her. See you."

Chapter Nine

Aaron Horwitz hurried up the passageway of an immense ocean liner, desperately searching for the steps that led to the deck above. He was late for his appearance as the main attraction in the ship's ballroom, but something grasped his arm and he couldn't break free. Someone called his name from the main deck.

138

"Aaron. Aaron, its your father."

He pulled away, but he opened his eyes and squinted at the bright sunlight that flooded the bedroom of his Brooklyn apartment. Aaron's roommate stood next to his bed in his pajama bottoms. After five years of rooming with Eddie, Aaron was still amazed at how much Eddie looked like Paul Newman. Except that Eddie was over six feet tall, not five-three. Aaron pushed his dark bushy mane aside to find the red numerals of the clock on his dresser. It read ten thirty-six.

"Aaron, your father is calling from Cairo, wherever that is."

"Okay, man. Thanks."

He sat up and took the phone. When he did so, he found himself staring into the dark eyes of Aaron Horwitz in the mirror. The eagle's beak of a nose and thick black eyebrows that met just above it gave him a sinister look that sharply contrasted with the young man's nature.

"Hi, Dad."

"Hello, son. Sorry to wake you. I never know when to call, with your schedule and all."

The familiar voice was clear enough to be coming from the corner drugstore. Aaron's parents had been divorced since he could remember, but his father had always called regularly, sometimes from places that Aaron could not pronounce. David Horwitz worked for the State Department.

"It's okay, Dad. We played until pretty late, and Eddie had a tough time getting me awake."

"How's the band doing?"

"We're doing fine. Could be better. We're not rich and famous, yet."

"Whenever you're ready to return to school, just let me know. I'll talk to the dean again."

"You always say that, Dad. You've never even heard us play. We're good. We just need the right break."

"Okay, Aaron. I know you're good. I just want the best for you."

139

"I just wish you'd come home and hear us some-time. I just need...oh, never mind."

"I know, son.   I will.   The next time I'm in Washington, I'll fly up. Soon."

"Okay, Dad."

There was a pause.

"Aaron?"

"Yeah?"

"Are you still dating Lisa?"

"Sure, why?"

"Isn't she in school in St. Louis?"

"Yes, but she was home for three weeks during the Christmas break, and she'll be back for spring break in March."

"How're she and Rachel?"

"Good. Doing very well. Why?"

"Oh, I'm just curious. I guess I just feel respon-sible for them since I helped them get into that program last summer."

Aaron sipped the coffee that Eddie had handed him.

"Rachel has a crush on some guy she met last summer. Had him up for Christmas, he and his buddy."

"What were they like?"

"A couple of farm boys from North Carolina. At least that's what we thought at first."

"Did you spend any time with them?"

"Yeah, as a matter of fact we put 'em up. The big guy, the friend, handled himself real well. Turned out that his mother is in the clothing business down in their little hick town and she comes to the city frequently on buying trips. Graham, that's the big guy, said he's been coming to New York with his mother since he was a small boy. Hard to believe he was ever small."

"What's he like, this Graham?"

Aaron paused.

"Is that why you called?"

"I'm not following you."

140

"You always get that tone when you're lying. Come on, Dad, this is me, the product of your genes. These dudes are a part of your special program and you're checking on your investment."

"Aaron..."

"Tell your friends they blew it. These guys are a bunch of sickos. They'll blow up the White House before they're done."

"Come on, son. I called to check on you. How's your cash situation? Need a loan or anything?"

"No, thanks all the same."

"I want you to visit me in Paris again. Or maybe Athens this time....I'm serious."

"Just let me know."

"It'll be soon, very soon.... Son?"

"You want to know about Graham and your other boy wonder, right?"

"Aaron, come on. Listen, did you guys drink a lot? I mean, did Graham exhibit any weird behavior after you guys had had a few?"

"No, Dad. These are just two regular dudes, as far as I could see. This Henry, he's a real jokester. He hit it off with everyone. A real charmer. Both of them, really. Who are they, Dad? Why are they in that program?"

"Need to know. Sorry."

"I'll ask Lisa."

"Good luck... So, no unusual behavior. Was there an incident in the park?"

"Who have you been talking to? These guys must be red hot. If they're being followed, why did your friends ask you to call me?"

"We just know there was an incident. Did many people see it?"

"It was nothing. Nobody noticed anything. One of the smalltime vendors approached us and offered his services in getting anything we wanted. Then he fell down. When he tried to get up, he couldn't. He laid some choice words on us, but he couldn't stand up. So what?"

"That's all?"

"That's it. What did you hear?"

"Look, I called to check on you. Thanks for your patience."

"Sure."

"Take care, son. Give my regards to your mother."

"Will do... Dad?"

"Yes?"

"Do you have a bodyguard or something?"

"Something like that."

"Have them check under the hood before you start up your car, okay?"

"These guys know what they're doing. I'm safer where I am than you are in New York. But thanks for the concern."

"I'll talk to you soon."

"Adios."

Aaron hung up and remained seated on the edge of his bed, thinking about Graham and Henry and the week they spent in the apartment. He had liked the boys from Carolina from the moment he met them. In fact, he had never seen strangers who were accepted so readily by his fellow band members and who fit in so easily with his friends. What a zany pair. Aaron knew why Rachel was attracted to Henry. What a funny guy. He liked being with Henry and the twins. It had been a fun week. They had been to the top of the World Trade Center and to the Museum of Modern Art, strolled through Central Park in the snow, sat through *Les Miserables*, and enjoyed a cold beer in each of numerous neighborhood taverns.

His band played twice while the tar heels were in town, and their enthusiasm for the music seemed genuine. At the Blooms' dinner party for their extended family, the visitors from down south were a hit once again. Aaron was surprised that no one seemed to mind that Rachel was dating a Gentile.

"Aaron, you wanna meet the others for breakfast?"

Eddie called from the other room.

"Sure, man. Hang on."

Aaron rinsed his face and squeezed a measure of toothpaste on to his brush. What was it about those two that made them eligible for that government program that the twins belonged to? He had known about the telepathic powers of the two girls for a long time. He never thought about it much until this government thing came along. How did the tar heels fit into the picture? Why was his dad so interested? What did his dad do for the government, anyway? He decided to call Lisa that night and ask her. If she wouldn't tell him anything, he'd understand.

"Let's go, man, they're waiting."

"Hang on, man. I'm coming."

Chapter Ten

Spring break at NC State was the second week in March. It coincided with that of Washington U. Henry flew to New York to join Rachel there. Graham decided to spend the week in Masonboro with his mother. On Monday evening Art called to ask Graham to visit Murphy High School to speak to the physics class.

"Frank Dawson, our principal, asked me about you. He had been talking to his physics teacher. She asked me to call and invite you to our school. She wants you to come and talk to her students and help some of them with their science projects."

"Sure, Art. It'll give me something to do. When do you want me?"

"Can you come on Wednesday?"

"What time?"

"She needs you at 9:30 and again at 1:15 if possible."

"No problem."

"Maybe we can have lunch? And maybe take a look at some of my students' art work?"

"Sure. I'll see you there. Have you heard from

Henry?"

"Not a word. We would have heard from Miss Bloom if he hadn't arrived safely. He'll be fine. After all, you guys learned to handle yourselves last summer. Right?"

"Need to know, Mister S."

"Okay, Graham. By the way, you can ride with me and spend the day with us, if you like. I'll be returning around four or four-thirty."

"No, thanks. I'll just drive over. See you there."

"Thanks for helping us out. I'll see you Wednesday."

Graham made the drive from Masonboro to Barclay in less than thirty minutes. It was an easy drive on a four-lane highway, and the school was located on the west side of town so it was not necessary to drive into downtown. Murphy was newer than Masonboro High, and Graham liked the way the campus looked. The red brick single story building was surrounded by evergreens, budding hardwoods, and fruit trees in bloom. The neatly edged sidewalks were lined with several varieties of shrubbery. Inside, sunlight flooded the entrance hall, and the receptionist in the front office, unlike Mrs. Clark at Masonboro, was pleasant and eager to help. Frank Dawson was away at a meeting, but a young physics student appeared to escort the guest through what seemed like several miles of sparkling locker-lined corridors to the science department. There he received a warm welcome from the physics teacher and her students.

Graham's visit was a success. He spoke about career opportunities in science and about contemporary issues such as cloning and other applications of DNA research, space exploration, and recent archaeological discoveries. He discussed individual ideas for projects and career paths with the students that gathered around him until late in the afternoon. When their time ran out, the teacher asked him to return the following day to spend time with the students who had been turned away. Graham thought that he should be embarrassed to play the role of the wise old sage after only one year of college, but he was having fun. He liked talking to others who loved science as much as he did. He promised to return the next day.

One of the students that he was able to help the next day was Calvin Dawson, a senior who happened to be the principal's son. Calvin was working on a computer project dealing with the mathematics of placing satellites in orbit. The two had met before, and each had a negative impression of the other. Now they couldn't remember why they hadn't hit it off.

"You're going to be a Wolfpacker? Engineering?"

"Design."

"No kidding. Where're you planning to live?"

"I don't know. I applied for a dorm room."

"You want to live in our suite at Sullivan? Tenth floor."

"Sounds good."

"I'll see what I can do next week."

Calvin's father found them in the science lab after school. He had come by to thank Graham for his visit.

"We haven't had this much excitement in the science department since some girl caught her hair on fire several years ago. Why don't you consider a career in education, young man? The pay's not great, but we have lots of fun," Frank said.

"Thanks. I'll think about it. I've enjoyed talking to Calvin. Does he get all his brains from his father?"

"What little there is comes from Mom," said Calvin, "And my height, too."

"Where does your size come from, Graham?" asked Frank. "Is your father a big man?"

"He's dead. From Lou Gehrig's disease. Several years ago."

"I'm sorry."

"Actually, Mr. Dawson, I was adopted. I don't know much about my genetic history."

"Sorry, again. I didn't mean to pry..."

145

"Leave it to the principal. Mister Sensitivity," said Calvin.

"Hey, it's okay. I had great parents. In fact, they say I look like my mom. She's pretty tall."

"She runs McGuire's at the mall, doesn't she?" asked Frank.

"Yep. I practically grew up in the back room when she was down on Ninth Street."

"Calvin's mother gets over to Masonboro and does some business with your mother about once a month. She has bought some fancy outfits there."

"Thanks."

"By the way, Graham. We've invited Art and his family to our new place at Bald Head Island for the Easter break. Why don't you and Henry come down for the weekend?"

"Yeah, man. It's really an exciting place," said Calvin, rolling his eyes.

"It's quiet and peaceful, Graham." Frank looked at his son. "Don't listen to Mister Big Time here. Its not Times Square, but we have a lot of fun."

"It sounds great. I'd like to see it. We'll try to be there."

Chapter Eleven

The Sandersons spent the last three days of the Easter vacation at Bald Head Island with the Dawsons. Frank was anxious to show Art his new house there, and Sharon and Anne, though they did not live in the same town and did not see each other very often, had been friends for years. The Dawsons had been on the island the entire week, and Art, Anne, and Greta, the youngest, joined them on late Thursday. Alexis stayed in Chapel Hill. Henry and Graham caught the eleven o'clock ferry Friday morning. They stood on the second deck as they glided past the Southport Marina and the waterfront restaurant on the port side, with the sparkling white homes on the main street in the distance. When the boat entered the river, the pilot opened the throttle, and the vessel surged forward. As one, the passengers braced against the wind and shouted to one another over the roar of the engine.

"This is nice," Graham remarked, with a serious expression on his face. "And the boat ride is, too."

Glancing around, Henry spotted the shapely young mother with the two-year-old son down below. She was the object of young Graham's comment.

"Her husband is probably 6-11 and three hundred pounds."

"And probably carries a double-barrel shotgun."

"You hungry?" asked Henry.

Henry knew what his friend's reply would be. Big Man was always hungry.

"Getting that way. Calvin told me there was a convenience store with a deli in the back where they make pretty good sandwiches."

"Maybe we should check with the folks first. They may have whipped up something."

"Probably a good idea."

The boat slowed to avoid creating a large wake as they passed a fishing boat.

147

"Henry?"

"That's my name. One of 'em."

"Do you know anything about Calvin?"

"Not really. Except he is one smart joker. His dad is great. Why?"

"I don't know. He seems okay, don'tcha think?"

"Sure. We'll know for sure next fall. I'm glad you asked him to live in the suite. He'll make Tommy a good roommate."

"I was impressed with him that day at your dad's school. He's called me a couple of times since."

"Are you sayin' you want to dump me and room with him?"

"No, but what would you think about telling him? It's going to be hard to keep it from him next year. It would make things a lot easier."

Henry swung around and stared at his friend.

"Are you crazy? You know what our orders are."

"Are you going to call McMann and tell him?" asked Graham.

"No, but..."

"Henry, this thing is growing. I feel so powerful. I don't know how far it's going. I'm thinkin' I need somebody else I can trust. A new set of eyes. A new perspective."

"So now I'm chopped liver."

"No, dummy. What I need is another one just like you. Two Henries. Three heads are better than two, you know."

"You don't really know anything about this kid. And that's all he is, a high school kid."

"Look, old boy. We already agreed that he could live in the suite with us next year. He'll either find out about me then, or we'll be forced to be even more restrained than ever."

"We can make a decision then. We don't need to do anything hasty."

"Hellfire, man. The boy is exceptional. He's okay. It's my secret. I've got to carry it around with me every day

148

like a big piece of luggage. The kid is a scientist. I just want to see how he reacts and hear what he has to say. You worry too much."

"You don't worry enough. You think this is all a joke."

"Will you just try to see things from my perspective? I walk around with the weight of this thing on my back constantly. No relief in sight for the rest of my life, as far as I know. And then, what does my number one man do? He adds to the burden. Always reminding me not to do this or that, don't say the wrong thing, keep the thing bottled up. Security precautions, for our own good, you say."

"That's my role."

"Says McMann. Look, man, I need friends who can loosen up and have some fun with this thing."

"Well, hell, lets check him out. If you feel good about him, I'm with you. Is that what you want me to say?"

"You are a hard-headed man, Cuz. Just wait. You'll see what I mean."

The boat left Cape Fear and entered the narrow inlet that led to the harbor. The day was warm and damp, overcast. A light maritime drizzle had not dampened the spirits of the passengers. They were greeted by a towering figure in glistening yellow raingear who waved from the walkway on the starboard side next to the channel. Henry recognized Calvin at once, even though they had not seen each other in at least two years. Neither of the three noticed the unremarkable man in the UNCW baseball cap, wind-breaker, and cream-colored cotton slacks who had worked his way around the deck and up the stairs to a position at the rail near Graham and Henry.

Chapter Twelve

Graham was right, Henry was forced to admit. Calvin turned out to be bright, sincere, thoughtful, and, most important, very funny.

Calvin had not realized how lonely he had been, up until now. He had been more than impressed by Graham when the college student had visited Murphy High; he had been amazed. How could a small-town boy from eastern North Carolina be his intellectual equal? And, at the same time, be a modest, down-to-earth dude who recognized Calvin's talent without a trace of envy. And who would believe his sidekick, a real character, was the son of Calvin's favorite teacher?

Later, Calvin and Henry would recall the urging of both their fathers for the two to get acquainted. Each admitted that he didn't like the idea primarily because it was his father's idea.

Late that afternoon they boarded one of the golf carts, and Calvin gave them a tour which included a climb to the top of Old Baldy, the lighthouse, and a stroll around the nature trail in the edge of the marsh. Then they pulled off Stede Bonnet to park next to the golf course and enjoy a couple of Rolling Rocks from Graham's cooler. That night they walked several miles along the beach. It was Saturday morning when Graham shared his secret with Calvin.

Chapter Thirteen

The house on Muscadine Wynd was the fulfillment of Frank Dawson's lifelong dream. After all those places he had rented by the week, at Nags Head and Emerald Isle and Wrightsville Beach, he had finally "jumped off the cliff", as they say in Japan, and bought his own place. He knew it was cheaper to rent, and he knew that it cost a lot more to build on the island because all the materials had to be brought over on a barge. But they had done it anyway. The new home, a four-bedroom, three-bath two-story stood on a private lot in the forest a short walk to the ocean and a few feet from a view of the marsh. Four twenty-five and some change, plus all new furniture and accessories. Of course they would have to rent it to help pay for it. The rent was eighteen hundred per week, and the agency already had it booked for a week in June and two in July.

Frank's favorite activity on the island was watching the sunset or listening to the nocturnal sounds of the semi-tropical forest from his favorite chair in the screened porch out back, enjoying a cocktail with old friends. He and Art the Artist were doing just that on that balmy April night when they heard the laughter of the boys as they drove up. Frank and Art had been talking politics, a favorite topic of each. Both men were Democrats, and they were in agreement on most issues.

"You can't discuss politics with Republicans," Art was fond of saying, "They're too hard-headed. If they were open-minded, they wouldn't be Republicans."

The boys came around the house and took the swing and two of the rockers on the end of the porch. Frank was pleased that they seemed to get along so well. Calvin needed new friends. He had outgrown that little clique he ran with back home.

"We were just talking about Slick Willie, boys. Henry, Graham, has the military forgiven him for dodging the draft and allowing gays to stay in? Or are they still bad-mouthing their commander-in-chief?" asked Art.

The cousins looked at one another, and Henry replied, "We never hear it discussed. Not in class, any-way. And we weren't around military personnel outside classes."

151

"What kind of program did you guys join?" asked Frank.

"It's an FBI training program. They want us to join the Bureau when we graduate. If we do, we'll have part of the training behind us. We'll hit the ground running, so to speak."

"Excuse me. I'm thirsty." Graham stood and opened the door. "Do you mind if I have some more orange juice?"

"Of course not," Frank replied. "Calvin, show them where the cups are."

All three of the young men headed for the kitchen.

"I hope Calvin can keep those guys out of trouble next year," Art said.

"They'll be the ones doing the baby-sitting. I'm glad they are making this connection. Calvin needed a new set of friends."

"And those two needed someone with a different point of view. Lord knows, Henry doesn't listen to me if Graham is around. Which is most of the time."

"Calvin is excited about NC State. It's a good school," said Frank.

"I never thought I'd have one of mine at Cow College," said Art.

Chapter Fourteen

Calvin was hungry. He needed a bath. He had a headache. He rose and paced to the window in the waiting room on the third floor at Wake Memorial Hospital. He had been there since he rushed to the emergency room three days before, minutes behind the ambulance that brought Candice. Candice had tumbled down a flight of steel-and-concrete steps as she was leaving Harrelson Hall, the round classroom building at the center of the NC State University campus. She had suffered a broken jaw, broken arm, and a chipped tooth. The gash on her head had re-quired twenty-six stitches, and she had scrapes and bruises

152

the length of her body.

Calvin had spotted Candice at the Wake Forest football game on a Saturday afternoon in mid September. He had not seen her since those three days at Bald Head Island, and he had not expected to see her at an NC State football game. She and two female friends were making their way up the steps to the exit at half time. Shouting, he made a frantic attempt to catch up to her, but the crowd spilled out into the aisle, making it impossible to exit the stadium until the fans around him did so. When he finally reached the concessions area, he raced to the nearest ladies' restroom and waited for the three girls to emerge. They never did. He spent the last half of the game searching the seats, to no avail. Finally, he returned to his seat and watched the Wolfpack complete their demolition of their long-time rival from Winston-Salem.

After the game and the drive in heavy traffic back to the main campus, Calvin searched the new student directory he found in a suitemate's room and found a Candice Brock listed at an apartment on Avent Ferry Road. It was late that night when he finally reached her. They talked until early morning.

"Why didn't you write me in France?"

"I don't know. I got your letter and it sounded like you were kind of busy. And I didn't know if the mail would reach you before you returned to Charlotte."

"I guess I was pretty busy. And distracted." She didn't want to tell him about Antoine.

"I guess North Carolina was a little on the dull side after a summer in Europe."

"A little. I thought about you, though. I started to call a couple of times, but I just didn't."

"I know. Charlotte seemed like a long way away. I actually called you once. I got the answering machine and hung up," Calvin said.

"I can not believe that you are a student here. What about Duke?"

"I got accepted to the school of design with a full

scholarship so I took it. What about you? What about Oberlin and Salem, those all-girls schools with no competition from men?"

"I took up a new hobby this past year...flying. I'm here on an Air Force ROTC scholarship. I plan to fly commercially when I get out of the Air Force."

"That's exciting. I'm happy for you."

"Calvin, are you going to ask me out?"

He did. And they had seen each other almost every day for more than a month. The accident had occurred during the first week of November.

Calvin pushed the button at the elevator. He had decided to go down to the coffee shop while Mrs. Brock was with Candice. When the door opened, however, Henry and Graham appeared and handed him a bag from Wendy's.

"How is she, man?" asked Henry.

"She's going to completely recover. No real harm done except a few scars. Both physical and emotional."

"That's great news, Cal."

"Has she talked about it?"

"She was tripped. She's positive."

"Why?"

"Who in the hell knows? Whoever it was cost her an entire semester of work. Not to mention the medical bills and the wear and tear on her parents."

"Are they with her now?"

"Her mom. One or the other has been at her side since they got here yesterday morning."

"Then you can get out of here for a while. You need some rest, man."

"It was Darnell Parker," said Graham. "It had to be. I should have taken care of that creep. He gave us fair warning. I should have put him out of commission."

When Henry turned, the look on his cousin's face sent a chill down his back and that made him shudder slightly. Calvin was starring at him, too, wide-eyed, reflecting.

"Come on, G.W., you're taking a gigantic leap. We

haven't heard a peep from that little prick since that night at the dorm. He's probably doing a big business over at Duke or Meredith or somewhere and has forgotten all about our little run-in." Henry was almost pleading.

"Nope. This is a message. And he's going to get a reply."

Darnell Parker was a small-time drug dealer from over in Durham who did business on college campuses in the Triangle area. Parker's business associate, a pale, stoop-shouldered young man with shaggy dark hair and baggy pants, known on the street as L.G., had been doing a little business in Sullivan Dormitory. When he appeared on the tenth floor, however, he was to learn that this was a mistake, for this was the home of our three heroes, two of which had recently returned from training that included how to deal with the likes of Mr. L.G.

Graham had wasted no time in challenging the young man, a pathetic figure in an over-sized athletic jacket.

"Whacha got in the pockets, asshole?"

"Whatd'ya need, man? Name it."

He sounded confident, but he took a step back, toward the elevator behind him. He was standing on the narrow balcony that ran the width of the building. Several curious students had stepped out of the suite next door.

Graham reached out and grasped L.G.'s jacket in a cat-like movement. He pinned the smaller man against the four-foot retainer wall that separated the walkway from a ten story drop.

"What I need, punk, is for you to get your carcass on that elevator and get out of this dorm. The next time I see you, your butt is going over the side."

He shoved L.G. to the floor and snatched the jacket over the young man's head. As he ripped the pockets, packets of powder and bottles of capsules tumbled to the concrete floor.

L.G. picked himself up and headed for the elevator. Turning, he shouted, "You're gonna be sorry for this, man.

155

I got friends that are gonna make you pay for that stuff."

L.G. soon found that he was the one who had made a mistake. His body surged forward and he skidded along the concrete, coming to rest before the elevator. A circle of students stood and watched as L.G. slowly picked himself up and stumbled into the elevator.

* * *

Exactly six nights later Darnell Parker and two menacing accomplices, dressed in black leather jackets, waited for Graham and friends at the entrance of Sullivan Dormitory. Darnell, a handsome young African-American in his early thirties with a small afro, adorned with gold on his neck and left ear and jewels on almost every finger, stepped forward and spoke in a soft voice. He was only five-seven or five-eight with a medium build, but his companions, both shaved bald, were much larger. On his right was a lanky, big-boned man with high cheek bones on a long sour face that was several shades lighter than those of his comrades. He was several inches taller than Graham, and he had the largest hands Henry had ever seen. The second companion stood six feet tall and almost as broad, his dark countenance covered with a heavy beard. Three sets of designer sunglasses hid their faces.

"Excuse, me, Calvin, Graham, Henry, I'd like to speak to you all for a minute."

"How do you know us?" Henry asked, startled.

"Well, I'm a friend of a young man by the name of L.G., and I understand you and him had a misunderstanding the other night."

"There was no misunderstanding. He was told to get off this campus and stay off. What do you want?" Graham's voice rose.

Henry could feel his own adrenaline flowing, not from fear of the intruders, but from dread of his cousin's awesome powers unleashed. And yet, there was a warm, reckless feeling in his own heart of hearts, one of power, secure in the knowledge that they could face down these bullies without fear.

"Look, GRAY-HAM, there's no need to be disrespectful. Young L.G. was not bothering anyone the other night. He does a little business around here. You need to leave the boy alone. Like I say, he's a friend of mine."

By this time a few passersby, overhearing the conversation, paused to witness more of the show.

"I tell you what, Darnell. You picked the wrong boys to come over here and try to intimidate. We don't scare. And I'll tell you like I told that other piece of trash, you take your poison, whatever it is, and you go pedal it on some other campus. We don't want you here."

Darnell bristled, but by this time a score or more witnesses were on the scene, and his companions had restrained the smaller man and were muttering that it was time to depart.

Someone in the crown shouted, "You tell 'em, Graham."

Another added, "Go home, drug dealers."

Darnell allowed his bodyguards to lead him away, but at the corner he turned and revealed the depth of his outrage. "If I was you guys, I'd call home every night from now on. Check on Frank and Sharon and the two girls. And Art, teaching away at old AD Murphy."

"Crawl back under your rock."

By this time, the three had reached the parking lot. Darnell continued to shout from his automobile, "And McGuire's dress shop in Masonboro, run by a little old lady named Janice. Tell her to watch herself."

Graham was seething. Henry had his arm in a vise-grip.

"Let 'em go, G.W. We won't see them around here anymore."

Now it was a month later, and they had not seen or heard from L.G. or Darnell in all that time.

"It was him. He was bluffing about Masonboro. If he had been there, he would have known that Janice was

157

not a little old lady. But Candice was here. It was a message to us."

"I don't care what happens to me. I'm going to kill those scumballs," Calvin said quietly.

"Do you mind having some help?" asked Graham.

"Hold on, boys. This is a job for the police," said Henry.

"What're you gonna tell 'em? That we've got a hunch we know who did it?"

"Why not? They can question Darnell and his bodyguards."

"You're dreamin', Henry. I'll take care of it. I'm not asking you guys to risk gettin' hurt. It's my girl-friend," said Calvin.

"Hold on, now, old buddy. Stop and think. We can nail these creeps without laying a finger on 'em. All we need is some inside information about their habits so we can catch up to 'em at the right time and place," said Graham.

Henry shook his head. "You guys are frightening me. We can not be having this conversation."

"Henry, they hurt an innocent girl. They're gonna pay."

Chapter Fifteen

"Hello."

"Rachel?"

"This is her alter ego, lover-boy. She's in the shower. Her first in two weeks."

"I can smell her from here. Smells like flowers in the spring."

"That's me you smell."

"Look, Lisa, I need to talk to her. It's important."

"Just tell me, Henry. I'll pass it along."

"Just have her call me, please."

"Henry. Listen to me. I'll pass it on."

"Oh. Okay. I need her help. No questions asked."

158

"She says no."

"Okay, okay. Here's the deal."

"Henry," Rachel interrupted. "I miss you. I think about you every day. How can I help you?"

"I miss you, too. Look, we need a favor."

"What is it, Henry-boy? You sound serious."

"You remember Calvin, our suitemate?"

"Sure."

"His girl friend was pushed down a set of stairs. She's in the hospital with a broken jaw, broken arm, and a bunch of stitches in her head. This character named Darnell Parker did it."

"Why?"

"Because she is Calvin's girl. Darnell is a drug dealer, and we ran him off the campus. We can't prove he did it yet. That's why we need some help."

"What can I do?"

"Do you think your bosom buddy, Captain Carla, would do you a favor, no questions asked?"

"First, it's Captain Lowe to you and me. She is a highly regarded member of... Well, you know who she is. Second, I wouldn't dare call and use my influence with her like that. Besides, what could she do?"

"All we want is some information on this creep. Address, arrest record, names of family and friends, stuff like that."

"Why?"

"We want to give the police a hand, but we can't just march into the police station and tell them that. We want to put a package together and drop it in their lap."

"What should I tell Captain Lowe?"

"Nothing. As little as possible."

"What if she wants details? Should I tell her it's for you?"

"Definitely not. That's the favor. Leave us out of it."

"Lisa doesn't like it."

"I'm asking you for a favor, not Lisa."

159

"We're just teasing. Of course we'll help you guys. I hope you nail the jerk. We'd like to be there to be in on the action."

"I wish you were here right now. God, I miss you."

"Transfer out here next year."

"You transfer to NC State....or UNC or Duke.

"Lisa says we should all transfer to Hofstra. We're homesick for the City."

"I can see why. It's a busy place. I like it there."

Chapter Sixteen

"Carla?"

"Who else would be on this secure line, Colonel?"

"Carla, You will receive a call from Rachell Bloom either tonight or tomorrow morning. She will request that you call the local police in Durham, North Carolina, for information about a small-time hood named Darnell Parker."

"This must be the work of our little rogues in Raleigh."

"You guessed it."

"How should I handle it, sir?"

"Okay, now, listen. I've talked to the man upstairs and he wants you to play along. Give the boys some rope. See how they handle themselves. To use his words, if we had tried to set up a test for them, nobody in our organization could have dreamed up anything this good."

"What's it all about?"

"This guy has pushed a friend of theirs down a set of stairs as a warning to them. Apparently they ran this Darnell, a local drug dealer, off campus a few weeks ago and he retaliated."

"How do they plan to use the information?"

"That remains to be seen. That's what interests us."

"Should I demand to know what it's all about?"

"Play it by ear. Be natural."

160

"Okay, Colonel, I'll handle it. Thanks for the warning."

"Captain?"

"Yes?"

"I know you're good. In fact, you're the best, but I still feel obligated to say this. I know you're attached to these kids...."

"They're a fine group of young people, sir. I think that anyone who..."

"All I'm saying is, be careful, Captain. These kids are smart as hell. If they ever found out just how close we were monitoring their actions and listening to their conversations, it would make our job ten times more difficult. I know I don't have to remind you how important our research is or how valuable the talents of these kids could be in the defense of this nation."

"I know, Colonel. You can count on me."

"You know I trust you, Carla. The man thinks you're the best. He sends his regards."

"Thanks, Colonel....Colonel, how many more are there?"

"Need to know, Captain. When you need to know, they'll share that information. I don't know either. There could be dozens, even hundreds. Although, I believe that this is a fairly new program."

"Well, thank you for the information. Good night, Colonel."

"Good night, Carla."

After she hung up, Carla went to the bathroom. As she returned to her living room, the phone rang.

Chapter Seventeen

"This is it, boys. I opened your mail, Cuz. I hope you'll forgive me. Here's your love letter, which I didn't read."

"The stuff on Parker?" asked Calvin. He had just spoken to Candice at her home in Charlotte where she was recuperating.

"Could I see it?"

The material had been faxed by the Durham police to Captain Lowe who had Fed-Exed it to Rachel in St. Louis. Rachel sent it to Henry in Raleigh, twenty miles from the Durham police station.

"Read for yourself," said Graham. "He did time as a minor, but it was purged from his record when he turned eighteen. Since then, he's been a suspect in dealing drugs and firearms and one murder case, but the only thing they've been able to pin on him is an assault on a female charge. He got two years probation for that."

"Here it is. Kisha Woodard. We need to call her."

"Is there a number?" asked Henry.

"No number, just an address."

"You boys ready for a little ride over to Bull City?"

Thirty minutes later they were in Durham watching Kisha Woodard's modest wood frame house through the windshield of Graham's SUV. The November sun had disappeared and the single street lamp on the corner was the only source light. They waited an hour before their patience paid off. As the slender African-American teenager emerged from the Woodard home and headed in their direction, Calvin stepped from the car.

"Excuse me, my man, lemme have a word witchu."

The young man started and half turned, poised to bolt to the safety of the darkness.

"What chu want?"

"I'm ain't here to hurt you. I want to talk a little bizness."

"Not interested." With that, he scampered back toward his home, his head twisted to keep an eye on the tall man in the darkness.

"Wait. It's not what you think. All I want is some information. I've got a twenty here just if you'll talk to me."

The boy paused and turned.

"Here," Calvin said. "I'll walk over to where you are. I don't mean you no harm. Stay right there."

162

"Okay. Le's see the money."

The youth took the bill from Calvin's outstretched hand.

"Do you know Kisha Woodard?"

"Never heard of her. Who wants to know?"

"How about Darnell Parker?"

"I don't know nothing, man. Here, take back the money. I got to go."

"Darnell beat up my girl friend. I'm out to get 'im."

"Darnell will shoot you dead, man."

"I thought you didn't know 'im."

"I don't. That way I stay alive."

"I got friends. We gon' take him down. We just need to know where we can find 'im."

"I wish you would. He beat my sister. For no reason but she lost his baby. She still got scars on the side of her face."

"What's your name, man?"

"Jamel Woodard."

"I'm Calvin. I live over in Raleigh. Here's another twenty to go with the other one. This piece of paper has my number on it. You think on it, and if you can think of a good place that we can catch ol' Darnell and hem him up, you call me."

Jamel accepted the money and the slip of paper and searched the smiling face of the tall man for some sign of deception.

"Oh, and Jamel?" Calvin had turned and started toward the car, but now he turned back toward the boy. "I didn't see you here tonight. In fact, I ain't never heard of any Jamel Woodard."

"Mission accomplished," muttered Calvin as he climbed into the car. "That's Kisha's brother. He's going to call me."

Jamel did not disappoint Calvin. He called three nights later, and they talked for thirty minutes.

163

Chapter Eighteen

That same night Doc's Tavern in downtown Fayetteville was the scene of a celebration of the discharge of Sergeant Harry Franklin from the United States Army. Some of the soldiers present were friends of Harry Franklin, but most did not know young Harry very well. They were there for the celebration.

"Harry, whatcha gonna do now?"

"Harry, I sure thought you would've re-upped again. Gung-ho as you always were."

It was true. Harry had been an exemplary soldier.

"Harry's got a job waiting for him up in Idaho."

"With who, Harry?"

Harry was normally a private young man, neat and orderly in his appearance, in his performance, and in his thinking. He was headed home tomorrow, to celebrate Thanksgiving in the little brick house on Dogwood Lane in good old Lynchburg. But he wished he didn't have to go. He dreaded watching his mother being treated like a slave by that loser that she married, the stepfather that had beaten and belittled Harry since he married Harry's mother when the boy was eleven.

Tonight he was not going to think about Lynchburg. Harry was celebrating. He had loosed his tie, and he was beginning to relax. His headache had almost gone. Harry was a lot more talkative when he had had a few.

"Whatcha got lined up, Harry?"

"I don't know if I have a job or not. You guys remember Sergeant Deitz? He told me to come to Idaho when I got out, and there would be a job for me. That was two years ago. Things could have changed by now. But what the hay, I've never been to Idaho."

"But Harry, the only thing you learned to do in the army was blow up things. What are you going to do out there in the middle of the forest, blow stumps out of the ground?"

Chapter Nineteen

Darnell Parker and his bodyguards could see the three puffs of breath that preceded them along the dark alley that led from the back door of the Starlite Lounge to Wilson Street where Parker's home and business office were located. The cold was good. It cleared his head. It was not quite two. Plenty of time to make his business appointment.

"Darnell!"

The three halted, mid-sentence, as three hooded figures emerged from the shadows.

"Time to pay your dues, Darnell."

"Who in the hell do you think you are?"

As one, the bodyguards reached for their weapons. The tall one's pistol flew from his hand and spun out into the night. The other, the possible professional fullback, was unable to control his weapon as it turned in his hand. The barrel jumped as it flashed and filled the air with light and sound. The tall one rose in the air and fell heavily to the concrete. Scrambling to his feet, he retreated into the darkness. The fullback's pistol jerked, swung in an arc, and struck his upper lip with a thud that echoed in the night. He groaned, and the butt of the gun struck him again, this time from behind.

A porch light of a nearby house was suddenly extinguished.

Darnell was shoved backward, and he landed heavily on his backside. The pistol in his fist, with a life of its own, slowly cocked itself and turned its barrel downward to press the muzzle against Parker's knee. He wailed in panic and shook his hand in an effort to release the weapon. The sharp crack of the shot pierced the air. He screamed and grasped his shattered kneecap. The pistol rose in the air and swooped down to thump the side of his head, then flung itself to the street, clattering into the gutter well out of the owner's reach.

From the dark the neighbors watched as the three

hooded figures turned and disappeared in the shadows of Wilson Street, the groans of Darnell Parker in their wake.

Chapter Twenty

The images of the evening played once again on Calvin's internal TV screen as he lay sleepless in spite of two hamburgers, a glass of milk, and a hot shower. The three had hardly spoken as Henry drove them back from Durham in his van. When they did, there was discord. Henry had expressed shock at Graham's harsh treatment of the three villains. Calvin could see the look on Candice's face when he saw her scars. He assured Graham that he had stopped short of what Darnell Parker deserved.

"We should have taken all three down to the beach and fed them to the sharks," he said.

"We should have disarmed them and turned them over to the police," Henry said. "We're not law enforcement officers. And we certainly aren't members of a jury."

Graham responded coolly, with the emotion of a computer on the university telephone answering system.

"Those men are hardened criminals. They're drug dealers, bullies, killers. They deserve worse than they got. The court system would have provided a lawyer for them and they would've been back on the street before we got back to Raleigh."

"What about the Constitution? Do your powers put you above the law of the land, Graham?"

"The people that wrote the constitution meant to protect the innocent, not the guilty. The Bill of Rights was not intended to handcuff the police to prevent them from protecting innocent people from the evil members of our society."

There was silence except for the whistle at the windows as the van sped though the cool November night.

Finally, Henry renewed the dispute.

"All I know is, if we give up the rule of law in this

166

country, all we have left is anarchy. Every man for himself. Might makes right, just like the old west."

"In the old west, when they caught a man rustling, they hung him on the spot."

"And how many innocent cowboys were hung by mistake? Or because someone accused them falsely?"

"Why is it preferable to sacrifice innocent victims by letting hundreds of criminals loose on the streets just to be sure that we don't occasionally punish somebody unjustly?"

They were silent once again. Henry slowed and turned right off Highway 70 onto Duraleigh Road. Calvin thought this could be the beginning of the end of their little club. An argument, a fight, a disagreement that could be resolved and forgotten was one thing, but this was a basic difference in philosophy.

Calvin's thoughts returned to the first weekend he spent with Graham and Henry. He had been delighted to have new friends to hang with, guys he could relate to. The thought of college in the fall excited him. To be invited by these zany new-found friends, to share their suite in the dormitory, was a dream come true. Almost too good a dream. He remembered having an uneasy feeling that something would come along to mess up his plans.

When the boys from Masonboro decided to reveal their secret during that weekend at Bald Head, Calvin had a hard time believing, even as he witnessed Graham's powers firsthand. Graham's first trick was to walk on water. As the three of them jogged down the beach in the surf, Graham veered away and tramped out into the ocean. Calvin attempted to follow, and he was up to his waist, then his chest before he paused and gasped, staring, dumbfounded. Graham plunged through the waves and beyond, circling, splashing, ankle-deep, laughing. Calvin turned to look at Henry who howled with laughter, pointing at Calvin. Calvin, puzzled, smiled sheepishly.

"This can't be happening," he muttered to himself.

Next came the slingshot trick. Graham stood,

hands at his side, as Calvin attempted to hit him with steel pellets launched from a slingshot from a distance of ten yards. The pellets swerved to the left or right, stopped and fell to the sand, or circled the target and returned to fall at the feet of the shooter.

On the drive home, the golf cart left the road by a few inches and increased its velocity threefold. The cart and three passengers literally flew though the forest, beer in hand, zooming past other carts that they encountered in the dusk.

Calvin demanded an explanation, and his new friends enthusiastically shared the whole story with him, eager to finally talk about the topic that was constantly on their minds but was a forbidden subject of conversation. They told it piecemeal, with each of the cousins interrupting the other with tales of half-forgotten incidents that set off new bouts of laughter and reminded them of more stories. The only part they held back was their involvement with the government, the summer training, and Colonel McMann. Calvin was dumbfounded. He had dozens of questions.

"Where did the gift come from?"

They didn't know.

"Who else knew? What about the family? How could all of you keep this secret for so long? When did you first know? Shouldn't Graham be tested by medical experts?"

When the initial shock was over, Calvin was in awe, overwhelmed with the thrill that Columbus or the Wright Brothers must have felt. Later he would feel gratitude that the cousins chose to share their secret with him.

That night they rode the golf cart on a strange journey up the Cape Fear River. The wet night air billowed past and the moon's reflection on the water just ahead led them as they sailed along, a foot above the water, then ten feet. The nuclear power plant, a gigantic Christmas tree, floated by on their port side. Further up the river they passed a ship, hardly visible but for a few navigation lights, tied up at the docks of at the Sunny Point Army Ammunition Terminal, the search light on the tower casting its circle of illumination on the objects it touched as it moved over the landscape. At the Brunswick Town state historic site, the cart floated above the stately live oaks to touch down on the lawn among the ruins of the colonial town. The three passengers disembarked to relieve themselves on the very ground where the inhabitants had defended their town from a Spanish attack in 1748 and where the British soldiers stood as they watched the town burn to the ground in 1776.

Chapter Twenty-One

"Colonel, I've just read your report on the incident in Durham. I wanted to call and congratulate you."

"Thank you, sir. I appreciate your taking the time to call." Colonel McMann spoke from his office in the Pentagon on a secure line. The caller was a superior somewhere up the chain of command, a man known only by a code name. A call from someone in the intelligence community higher than his immediate supervisor was rare.

"I sounds as if our boy handled himself very well."

"Yes, sir. We thought so."

"Colonel?"

"Yes sir."

"Put your best people on this assignment. The old man considers this boy one of the most important developments to come along in a long time."

"Yes sir."

"Make sure he understands how important he is to the country. And stress the need for security. And... I don't want to tell how to do your job, but if you can, let him know we are proud of his work down in Durham."

"Yes sir. I'm glad you suggested it. I'm having him flown up next month for a physical and a little pep talk."

"That's perfect. And I'd like you to read a case we're working on. You may want to involve the young man.

169

As an observer only. It's developing in his back yard. I'll leave it to you."

"Yes sir. He's ready for the next step."

"You'll have the file within the hour. Good luck."

"Thank you, sir."

Chapter Twenty-Two

Henry and Calvin sat in the locker room at Carmichael Gym and quietly pulled on their socks and shoes and dried their damp heads the last time before tossing their towels into the receptacle. They met at the athletic facility to play basketball two afternoons each week. They had played half-court, five-on-five, today, and they had been forced to guard each other, a task not relished by either. They donned their outer wear, Calvin in a topcoat and toboggan and Henry in his jacket over a sweat-shirt and hood, and headed for the doors on the north end. They met a dozen or more intramural players, many dressed only in shorts and tee-shirts, running and laughing, joining their teammates on their respective courts to begin their warm-ups.

Outside, the melancholy darkness made it seem later than 5:30.

"You want to stop and eat?"

"Might as well."

"You seen Warf?"

"Nope. He's probably somewhere studying for a physics test."

"Henry, does it bother you that you and Gray don't have much to say to one another?"

"Not really. We get along. You know that."

"Yeah, but it's not the same. I'm sorry, too. I miss how it was before Candice got hurt."

"I'm sorry about you and Candice, too. I saw you and her talking yesterday. Any chance you might get back together?"

"Naw. She just doesn't want to see me any more.

Those scars bother her, not me. But she doesn't want to listen."

They entered the noisy cafeteria and made their choices in the food line. They found a table in the corner and ate in silence until Calvin resumed the conversation.

"Henry, the truth is, Candice told me somethin' that has me a little upset. I know it shouldn't, but it does."

"What was it?"

"You know who she's been seeing? Your cousin and my best friend, none other than Superman himself."

"Damn. Are you sure?"

"She didn't want to tell me, but she wanted to clear the air."

"How long has this been goin' on?"

"Just two dates, this past weekend. But they're serious. She told me so."

"Well, Calvin, it's not like he dated her while she was going with you. You two hadn't been together since she got hurt, over a month ago."

"I know, but it still hurts."

"I'm sorry, man. You just need somebody new to take your mind off of her."

They cleared the table and stepped out into the first cold heavy drops of a winter rain.

"Calvin?"

"Yeah?"

"Has Graham told you about the government program that we belong to?"

"No, but I know you guys go somewhere for training in the summer. I figured you'd tell me when you wanted to, or when you could."

"Well, we can't. But I'm getting out of it. I talked to a man named McMann this week. He's going to get me into the Navy ROTC program over in Chapel Hill."

"Congratulations. I just can't picture you as a naval officer," Calvin chuckled.

"Me either, to tell you the truth."

They had reached the dorm, and they noticed that

171

only two of the three elevators were in operation. By the time one arrived, a capacity crowd was waiting to squeeze through the doors. They waited patiently as the car stopped at every floor.

"Come on and go to New York with me during the holidays."

"I sure would like to. My parents want their boy home for the Christmas break, though. Gray tell you he's going to DC?"

"Yeah. He's going to meet with McMann on his own."

"I hate to see you guys like this, man."

"Don't worry about it."

Chapter Twenty-Three

"Are you up for this, Harry?"

"Sure, Sarge, why not? You know I can handle myself."

Harry Franklin and Rodney Deitz, the burly retired Army sergeant seated next to Harry were bound for Raleigh-Durham as soon as their 747 was cleared for takeoff from Chicago's busy O'Hara Airport. Deitz's full beard and long hair, which he wore in a ponytail, were almost completely white. He and their companion, the tall, thin man who slept in the seat across the aisle, wore open collars and cotton slacks. It was the first time that Harry had seen either without their camouflage fatigues, military-style working caps, and combat boots. Nor had he seen them without some type of weapons.

"Well, you know how the boys are," said Deitz, glancing over at their companion. "Some of 'em think it's a little early for you. As a matter of fact, I agree with 'em, but you're perfect for this job. You know explosives, you know the Raleigh-Durham Airport, and you can handle yourself in a firefight. They all agreed to send you on my say-so."

"You won't be sorry, Sarge. I won't let you down."

"I hope not. When they asked me about how

172

strong your commitment is to what we're doin', I didn't know what to tell 'um. This ain't no boy scout cookout, they said, and they're right."

The two did not look at one another.

"I hope you told 'em that they could count on me to follow orders. That's the way I like it. You make the plans, and old Harry'll execute."

"That's exactly what I said." Deitz turned and looked into Harry's eyes and grinned. He looked ten years younger when he smiled.

He looked up the aisle for an attendant. "Let's see if we can get us a drink while Wes is asleep."

The three of them were making a dry-run mission in preparation for the real thing. They belonged to a radical anti-government organization called the Rocky Mountain Volunteers, and their target was the son of FBI chief K. Paul Maxwell. An undergraduate at Duke University, the young man was scheduled to fly to Washington out of Raleigh-Durham in two weeks.

"We're just gonna keep this guy for a few days and turn him loose?" Harry asked. The three were eating pizza delivered to their room at the Comfort Inn near the airport.

"Maybe shave his head, scare him a little. Mainly, we just want to send Mr. J. Edgar Hoover Maxwell a message," answered Deitz.

"What's wrong, Hotshot? The old backbone's not going mushy on us, is it?" asked Wesley Williamson, the third man. Wes looked mean when he wasn't grinning, but when he did, as now, he looked downright evil.

"No, I'm okay. I just want to have it all straight in my mind going into this thing," Harry answered. He paused, then his eyes met those of Williamson as he added, "Wes, if you don't think I can handle this job, why'd you wait until now to bring it up?"

Wes looked away, but he swung his legs off the bed and sat erect. He was a dour man, lean, almost thin, and hard. An expert marksman, he moved through the forest like a stalking cat. An ex-Marine, Wes had served in

173

the Volunteers for twelve years. He was a good man to have on your side when the going got rough. He directed his cold stare at Harry across the room.

"Hold on, Harry," Deitz said. He stood up.

"I did object," Williamson said. "I told 'em you were wrong for this job from the beginning."

"Now, hold on, Wes," Deitz tried again. "You're a new member, Harry. Wes and a number of others questioned the wisdom of bringing you along. They've never seen you in action, and this is a dangerous mission. You really can't blame 'em. It makes sense. Now I served with you and know what you can do and I said so and the council voted to put you in the operation. Wes and the boys are goin' along with it, but they don't necessarily like it."

"I know all that, Sarge. I just get tired of all the lip."

They were interrupted by two knocks on the door, a pause, and two more.

"That'll be Snow."

Williamson opened the door cautiously and admitted a short, heavy-set, fifty-year-old man with a white mustache, a red baseball cap, and dark glasses. Snow glanced nervously behind him as he entered.

"You guys ready?"

"You have everything?" asked Deitz.

"I got it all. We'll go look at it now, then we'll go somewhere safe and talk. Wes, you come with me, and we'll pick you two up around the corner by the ice machine."

The three men did as they were told, and within a few minutes they were on the interstate headed east.

Chapter Twenty-Four

The next few weeks were filled with hard work for the three friends at NC State. The rift loomed in the background. The cousins remained close, but their best efforts to return to the days of old were not successful.

174

Their studies kept them apart much of the time. They spent some time together on weekends, but Graham began to spend more time with Candice. Graham had tried to clear the air with Calvin, and Calvin claimed to be understanding, but the look in his eye told a different story. Now Graham tactfully avoided mentioning Candice at all.

Henry had seen his cousin and the girl together several times, once in a restaurant and twice in local night clubs. The contrast of the two, Graham tall, blond, broad-shouldered, and Candice, short, her shining flesh dark as midnight, her short hair and stylish clothes that never quite concealed her ample womanhood in all the appropriate places, turned heads wherever they went. The attention they drew was apparently ignored by both. They seemed totally focused on each other. Candice, her white teeth glistening, her eyes flashing, was truly a beautiful woman, and the scars on the right side of her face served only to make her appearance more intriguing. Seeing the two together made Henry feel happy.

Henry and Graham had discussed Henry's plans to swap the spy business for the Naval ROTC program in the spring. He would graduate an Ensign and serve four years active duty. Strangely, each seemed relieved.

Graham was flying more at night on his own. He hardly ever used the elevator anymore after dark. Frequently he appeared, tapping at their window on the tenth floor, waiting for Henry to open the window. Calvin dubbed him Batman.

Graham was taking flying lessons, courtesy of Uncle Sam and the taxpayers, much to the relief of Henry and Calvin. He needed to learn to fly because he was flying everywhere he went. They flew the Warf family Jeep Cherokee to Myrtle Beach the first week of Christmas Vacation. The lights of the occasional aircraft above them and the power lines followed along in the darkness below them made Henry and Calvin nervous.

Henry dreaded to see Graham drinking. He feared that the public and the press would discover his secret though some careless act on Graham's part. If they did, it would be necessary for Graham to remain in seclusion for the rest of his life. Just like Bruce Wayne. And Clark Kent.

Graham and Henry no longer discussed Graham's role in the military. On one hand, Henry was sorry that he could no longer lend support to his long-time comrade, but on the other, he was glad that he was no longer required to communicate with Colonel McMann and his cloak-and-dagger associates.

Graham now carried a secure cell phone which gave him a 24-hour hookup with Washington, and he was away from the campus frequently during the day. Henry imagined that he was at the local FBI office or in some secret room in the Federal Building, receiving instructions for his next mission.

Chapter Twenty-Five

Christmas was a happy occasion at the Sanderson house that year. Graham and Janice were there, and Calvin drove over from Barclay for the noon meal. Alexis brought her new beau, a second year medical student from West Virginia. He was a handsome young man who seemed to feel comfortable with her family. He was an inch shorter than Alexis when she wore heels. He didn't have much to say, due, perhaps, to the fact that Alexis didn't give him much of a chance. Henry saw why she liked him, though. He had an honest face and a nice smile.

Henry had either been on the phone or on line in a chat room with Rachel every day since the holidays began. He planned to fly to New York two days after Christmas. He had not been able to reserve a seat on a flight back to Raleigh on the Sunday after New Year's, but he would worry about that later. Something would come up. It always did.

At noon on Christmas, the Sandersons rode out to the family farm, which was now only ten minutes from the Masonboro city limits. They met at the home of Art's older

176

brother, a handsome two-story brick house that stood next to the more modest turn-of-the-century country home where Art grew up. His sister flew in from San Francisco, and his nieces drove down from Greensboro and Norfolk with their families.

Art's mother and her cousin, each in their seventies, did most of the cooking. There was turkey, a ham, a country ham, boiled potatoes, sweet potatoes, bean salad, two vegetable casseroles, butter beans, beets, fruit-and-jello salad, deviled eggs, watermelon rind pickles, plus bar-be-que, collards, and corn bread. For dessert they consumed a big part of four cakes, two pies, and a plate of brownies.

That afternoon almost all male family members and guests, including Art's 53-year-old brother and his brother's 10-year-old grandson, played touch football in the pasture next to the old home place, a family tradition that went back at least to Art's childhood. Greta and her female cousins from Norfolk decided to join in.

As they changed to sweat clothes and sneakers in the upstairs bedroom of the old home place, Henry and Calvin watched Graham and Alexis through the window. The two reached the curve of the farm path that led to the woods beyond the back field that had long been a favorite family haven for children's games, long walks, and private meditation over the years. Though Graham and Alexis were some distance away, the bursts of frosted air that they emitted as they spoke were still visible.

"Notice the heavy coats and gloves?" Calvin observed. "They'll be up in the air in ten minutes."

"Yep." Henry paused at the door. "But, you know, he'd much rather be playing ball with us."

"I know. I wish he could."

Chapter Twenty-Six

Jim, the future doctor from West Virginia, dropped Henry off at the Raleigh-Durham Airport the next day.

177

Alexis and Jim planned to pick Henry up when he returned from New York on the third of January. Alexis and Jim had insisted. They planned to be at the airport to pick up Jim's roommate, whose return flight was due that same Sunday afternoon, anyway.

"Just don't get snowed in, birdbrain. And don't cut your time to La Guardia too close. They'll sell your seat in a heartbeat. It's the busiest weekend of the year, you know."

"Yes, Ma'am, Miss Expert-on-Every-Damn-Thing. How do you stand it, Jim? Does she talk to you like that?"

"Well, ... yeah, I guess she does."

"Jim, he will always be my little brother. I do not talk to you that way."

"Whatever you do, I like it."

"Oh, man. Okay. I'll be at RDU on the third. Then we'll wait for the roommate from Philly."

Chapter Twenty-Seven

On the third of January, Harry Franklin, Rodney Deitz, and Wesley Williamson were back in Raleigh. This time they stayed at the Sheraton at Crabtree Valley Mall. They had landed at RDU in the middle of the afternoon, and when they checked in Deitz lay down to sleep off the drinks he'd had on the plane. Harry went next door to see if Wes wanted to walk over to the mall. Wesley declined to go and objected to Harry going out on his own.

"We're supposed to stay in our rooms, lie low for these three days, stay out of sight, don't take any chances. You don't listen too good."

"Come on, Wes. I need to pick up a couple of parts at Radio Shack, man, for, you know, spares. And I just want to wander around and look. It's crowded over there, man. I'll be invisible."

"Be back in an hour. And bring us back somethin' to eat. Somethin' good. I don't want no chicken sandwich. Bring us a steak and potatoes and some ice tea."

"Will do. It may take a few extra minutes to cook the steaks, though."

"Pretty Boy, I want you to listen to me real good."

Wesley's voice was high-pitched and extremely irritating. He reminded Harry of Bruce Dern.

"What is it?"

"I'm watchin' you real close. You may be Deitz's fair-haired boy, but you screw this mission up, and you ain't goin' back to Idaho. And when they finally start to find parts of you, they ain't going to be able to make a I.D."

"I'll do my part, Wesley. You just do yours."

Harry left the hotel and headed for the mall across the parking lot. He had an hour. That should be plenty of time. He looked forward to the day when he could give Wesley Williamson what he had coming to him. Soon.

Deitz was awake when Harry returned with the steaks. After they ate, they went over the plan, step-by-step, for the second time that day and at least the tenth time in the past two weeks. It was a daring plan. If it worked, the Rocky Mountain Volunteers would be a household word.

The objective was the kidnapping of Carter Maxwell, the youngest son of K. Paul Maxwell, newly appointed Director of the Federal Bureau of Investigation. An undergraduate student at Duke, Carter was scheduled to arrive at Raleigh-Durham Airport from Washington on January 6. The Volunteers planned to abduct him at the airport.

First, they would arrive at the airport in an RPS van, and, as Wes unloaded the vehicle, Harry was to deposit a briefcase containing a bomb on the luggage conveyor belt. In the chaos created by the explosion, the trio planned to subdue young Maxwell with a safe but effective chemical substance injected quickly into his arm or leg and load him into the van. At a remote parking lot on the airport property, they would change vans, drive through the gate, and proceed west on Interstate 40 to a truck stop in Burlington. There they would board a tractor-trailer for the drive to a secluded camp in northern Georgia. It was up to

179

their local accomplice, Eddie Snow, to have vehicles, weapons, explosives, and provisions in place as needed.

It was a risky operation, but the stakes were high. If successful, they could hold the United States government hostage while they made headline news daily. For the plan to work, they had to move swiftly, they had to avoid mistakes, and they needed to be lucky. First they must identify the target. Their intelligence was sketchy, primarily because they did not want inquiries about the young man to signal a warning to his father and his agents. They knew that he was six-foot-three or -four, and he frequently wore a Blue Devils baseball cap over short blond hair. A small earring hung from his left ear. Most likely he would be met by a tall female companion with a very dark complexion and jet-black hair whose ancestors were from India or Pakistan. They also had an ID card with a picture, two years old.

The next step would be to detonate the bomb at a location far enough from young Maxwell to ensure that he did not become a casualty. The bomb was a small one. The explosion would be loud and create a lot of smoke but casualties would be kept to a minimum. They did not intend to turn the public against them as the boys at Oklahoma City had done. The bomb was Harry Franklin's responsibility. Then there were the transfers in the parking lot and at the truck stop. They would need to move quickly without being noticed by bystanders. A witness who could describe their vehicle could bring the Highway Patrol down on them in a hurry.

Ex-Sergeant Deitz reviewed their plan step-by-step, item-by-item, his calm voice full of confidence, his manner as relaxed as if he were planning a birthday party. Only Snow appeared nervous. Harry was glad Snow would not be taking an active part in the operation.

"You just have everything ready when we need it, Eddie-boy, then you take that money and you bury it somewhere, and go crawl back under the hood of one of your cars and forget you know us," Williamson told him.

"Don't worry, boys. It'll be there."

"And keep that money hid for a year, remember?"

"I know, I know. I'll keep my part of the bargain. You guys just be careful."

At that moment, Alexis and Jim sat at the airport, waiting for the roommate from Philly. Henry had called to say he was staying another three days. Would they please call Mom and Dad? And could they please pick him up on the sixth?

Alexis had assured him that they would.

Chapter Twenty-Eight

On the sixth of January, Henry's flight from LaGuardia to RDU had been inexplicably delayed. He didn't mind spending more time with Rachel, but he wished he could have reached Alexis before she drove all the way out to the airport. Already the delay was almost an hour and a half.

Rachel and Henry had made a decision over the holidays. They planned to be married when they graduated in the spring of 2002. In the meantime, Rachel planned to transfer to NC State in the fall. They had decided to share an apartment in Raleigh during the final two years of college. Rachel called Captain Lowe with the news hoping for a sign as to how this development would affect Rachel's status with the government, but she was noncommittal. Henry suspected that it wouldn't matter that much since he had been a part of the program himself. She didn't want to leave the program, and he wanted her to have whatever she wanted. So they sat in the airport and watched the latest on the impeachment trial, and, like most Americans, they longed for an end to the Congressional proceedings and a return to the news of more normal times. Maybe a good swift air strike against Iraq's missile sites, or perhaps a people's demonstration in Indonesia.

Chapter Twenty-Nine

Alexis Sanderson drove to the airport directly from the shopping mall in Cary where she had searched for a birthday gift for her roommate. After discovering that her brother's flight had been delayed, she had purchased a magazine and ordered a cup of coffee in the lounge where she intended to wait. After more than an hour, she took a tour of the airport. She would visit the ladies' room, call her apartment for messages, and see if she saw anyone she knew. After all, people from all over eastern North Carolina flew out of RDU. She was downstairs near the baggage claim area when the airport security people came through, moving everyone upstairs. Customers, baggage handlers, ticket sales people, and bystanders were removed from the area. Alexis, thinking that a celebrity was coming through, ducked into the restroom and stood on a toilet in order to remove her feet from view.

Harry Franklin and his two companions entered the terminal at the baggage claim entrance thirty minutes later. All wore the striped uniforms of RPS delivery personnel. They seemed to notice no abnormal activity. Travelers waited by the baggage carrousel, baggage handlers waited for those who needed their services, and relatives and friends greeted incoming passengers. All were FBI agents, calmly playing their parts, some with a certain relish.

Agent Manosa, stationed behind the automobile rental desk alongside young Graham Warf, subsequently reported what she witnessed that day more than once. The first of the three terrorists stepped away from a small crowd of passengers and placed his briefcase on the carrousel. His companions, pushing a cart loaded with packages, lingered in the vicinity of the towering youthful agent clad in a Duke sweat shirt, a Blue Devils baseball cap, and a conspicuous cross swinging from his left ear. His hair was not quite blond, and there was no dark-skinned girlfriend, but the RPS agents seemed to take him for young Mr. Maxwell as planned. In the confusion of the activity in the room, agents had grabbed the briefcase in question and verified that it contained only a harmless smoke bomb. They were set to detonate, a signal that was to set both parties in motion, when, out of the ladies' room and on to center stage stepped a dark-haired beauty in black slacks that got the immediate attention of fifty male FBI agents. There she stood, bewildered, when the briefcase began to spew its bitter smoke. As the agents all over the room fell to the floor, Harry Franklin, in a flash, sprinted the few yards that separated him from the newcomer, later to be identified as Alexis Sanderson, and dove to knock her to the floor, pinning her under him. Harry was a student of history who believed that the future hinges on the pivotal junctions of luck and one's actions. This reflex that left him nose-to-nose with the sweet-smelling young Alexis, cousin of the extraordinary Graham Warf, was to change his life forever.

The rest happened in the space of a heartbeat. Deitz and Wilkerson drew machine pistols from their jackets, weapons that were immediately snatched from their hands as they were slammed to the floor by some unseen force. At the same instant, Harry Franklin rose in the air above where Alexis lay and flew though the glass door of the travel office to collapse unconscious in a bed of broken glass.

"He's ours, he's ours." Agent Manosa grasped Graham's arm, shouting in his ear.

Voices shouted in Manosa's ear set, "What in the hell is he doing? Manosa, stop him."

"He's killing his own men."

"Get him out of here."

"Who in the hell briefed him?"

Meanwhile, Wesley Wilkerson had managed to pull away from the agents that surrounded him and push though double doors, pursued by several agents. As he dashed to the rear of the RPS van, however, he flew into the air, feet first, and dropped, head first, and bounced on the top of the van. His unconscious body then slithered from the roof of the van to a tangle on the pavement at the feet of a dozen agents. They watched as Graham took his cousin into his arms.

Three ambulances had wailed their way to the scene and medical technicians persuaded Alexis to lay on their stretcher. When she heard Graham's outburst, however, she sprang to her feet.

"What do you mean, 'ours'? Why wasn't I told? You guys are unbelievable."

"I thought you knew, Warf. Who briefed you, anyway?"

"So that guy was taking Alex out of the line of fire. And I jacked him up for his trouble."

"Graham?"

He turned to take Alexis' hand.

"Is he going to be okay? I want to find him at the hospital," Alexis said.

"Do you have a car?"

"Henry's van."

"Lets go."

When Henry arrived from New York three hours later there was no one at the airport to meet him. He managed to catch the shuttle service to the Brownstone Hotel and, after a thirty minute hike and a ten minute wait for an elevator, he arrived at his dorm room in time to take a call from Jim the future doctor from West Virginia. Jim was looking for Alexis. Minutes later Candice called in search of Graham.

Chapter Thirty

The telephone woke Henry at 5:30 AM. A reporter from a local television station asked for Graham. Several minutes later, a reporter from the Associated Press called, also trying to locate Graham. By seven, there were five others.

Henry heard the whole story at eight when Graham arrived to bring Henry to the hospital. Alexis sat with Harry

Franklin as she had through the night. Harry had suffered a few minor cuts and a mild concussion and was due to be released the next day. He didn't attempt to hide the pleasure he took from Alexis' attention. To her, this handsome young agent had saved her life, and now she was bound to him.

No one knew the status of Harry's undercover assignment. That would be determined after an extensive debriefing at FBI Headquarters.

Chapter Thirty-One

Henry scanned the horizon as he made his way across campus. He had a feeling that he was being observed and that he soon would receive a visit from the sky. He was not disappointed.

"Hen-ry. Hen-ry."

The call came from above his head. Students froze, their mouths ajar, as a white Jeep Cherokee descended slowly and landed on the bricks a few feet from Harrelson Hall where Henry waited. He opened the door and crawled in. He was greeted by a mischievous smile Graham Warf saved for his most outrageous behavior. Henry was inside the vehicle before he noticed Calvin in the back, doubled with laughter. As dozens of amazed students watched, the vehicle silently rose to a comfortable altitude above the brick high-rise dormitories, spun, and surged toward the southeast. In a less than an hour, the trio was cruising down the Cape Fear River once again. They ate lunch in the restaurant overlooking the harbor at Bald Head Island.

"That's a weird bunch we work for...I work for, Cuz. I made a mess of the whole operation, almost killed our own man and one of the key witnesses, and what do they give me for it? A commendation. I fly up to have McMann introduce me to the Director next week."

I'm happy for you, Gray. You have an important gift. It's time you were recognized and put to your best use."

"No, you were right, Henry... about everything. I'm too hot-headed. I can't be above the law."

"I didn't say you were above the law."

"That's what it amounts to, and you know it. If I try to set myself above the law, sooner or later I'll be seen as an enemy of the law and an enemy of the nation."

"Bullshit."

"No, its true. And you know it."

"I need you for my moral compass, Henry. I want to be able to talk things out. Not every day, but a couple of times a month."

"Graham, I'm just going to sea in a couple of years. You can fly out in a few minutes from anywhere in the world."

"Thanks. I don't mean to sound corny. I just wanted you to know that I know that you were right. You were right about the secrecy and the publicity. Everybody and his brother saw what I did yesterday. I'm afraid I've brought a hailstorm of media down on you and Mom and our family."

"We'll stonewall."

"I'm leaving. I've ask them to transfer me to another school somewhere under a different name."

"You don't have to do that."

"I should have done it before now."

"Guess who else is leaving," said Calvin.

"What do you mean?"

"He's my new sidekick," explained Graham. "He's on the payroll. McMann loves him."

"Well, congratulations, Hotshot. You guys going to continue your education or will you be full-time G-men?"

"We'll go somewhere. Maybe Georgetown."

"Assumed names, I assume."

"Who knows. Leave it to McMann and company."

"And that cute little Captain Lowe."

"Cuz, I want you to square things for me with Candice. Tell Candice I'll call her soon, but she is not to

186

know my whereabouts. I'm afraid for her safety. My enemies could try to get to me through her."

"Say goodbye for me, too," said Calvin.

"Will do. When are you going?"

"Tonight."

"What about Janice?"

"She knows. I'll run by and see her again before we leave, but I want you to look out for her."

"You know I will." Turning to Calvin, Henry asked, "What about Frank and the girls? What do they think about all this?"

"They were overwhelmed at first, but McMann himself called on a secure phone they issued me. They want the best for me."

"That's good."

They watched the crew of the one o'clock ferry secure the boat and unload one load of luggage as a handful of passengers disembarked and rushed to find shelter from the January wind.

"I'll miss flying."

"We'll still do it. You just won't know when I'm coming."

"I hate to see you two go. Things won't be the same around here."

"I feel like I'm cutting off my arms and legs. Explain that to everyone, won't you?" Graham asked.

"Can I help you pack up your stuff?"

"Do you mind?"

"Let's go, Big Man. We'll park on top of the dorm."

ISBN 155395782-2

9 781553 957829